Holly in Love

CAROLINE B. COONEY

SCHOLASTIC INC.
New York Toronto London Auckland Sydney Tokyo

Cover Photograph by **Owen Brown**

ISBN 0-590-32558-2

12 11 10 9 8 7 6 5 4 3   4 5 6 7/8

Holly in Love

A Wildfire Book

WILDFIRE TITLES FROM SCHOLASTIC

Love Comes to Anne by Lucille S. Warner
I'm Christy by Maud Johnson
Beautiful Girl by Elisabeth Ogilvie
Superflirt by Helen Cavanagh
Dreams Can Come True by Jane Claypool Miner
I've Got a Crush on You by Carol Stanley
An April Love Story by Caroline B. Cooney
Dance with Me by Winifred Madison
Yours Truly, Love, Janie by Ann Reit
The Summer of the Sky-Blue Bikini by Jill Ross Klevin
The Best of Friends by Jill Ross Klevin
Second Best by Helen Cavanagh
The Voices of Julie by Joan Oppenheimer
A Place for Me by Helen Cavanagh
Sixteen Can Be Sweet by Maud Johnson
Take Care of My Girl by Carol Stanley
Lisa by Arlene Hale
Secret Love by Barbara Steiner
Nancy & Nick by Caroline B. Cooney
Wildfire Double Romance by Diane McClure Jones
Senior Class by Jane Claypool Miner
Cindy by Deborah Kent
Too Young to Know by Elisabeth Ogilvie
Junior Prom by Patricia Aks
Saturday Night Date by Maud Johnson
He Loves Me Not by Caroline Cooney
Good-bye, Pretty One by Lucille S. Warner
Just a Summer Girl by Helen Cavanagh
The Impossible Love by Arlene Hale
Sing About Us by Winifred Madison
The Searching Heart by Barbara Steiner
Write Every Day by Janet Quin-Harkin
Christy's Choice by Maud Johnson
The Wrong Boy by Carol Stanley
Make A Wish by Nancy Smiler Levinson
The Boy For Me by Jane Claypool Miner
Class Ring by Josephine Wunsch
Phone Calls by Ann Reit
Just You and Me by Ann Martin
Homecoming Queen by Winifred Madison
Holly in Love by Caroline B. Cooney

O^{ne}

It was cold enough to make a polar bear shiver. I stood at the bus stop listening to my blood, which I was quite sure had frozen solid and was now breaking up into icy little splinters, traveling like miniature red icebergs up to my heart valves.

I'm only seventeen, I thought, and I'm about to die of winter.

Kate came leaping and bounding over the snow. Her cheeks were rosy from the cold, and she didn't seem to notice the snow crawling down inside her boots each time she stepped in a drift. "Oh, Holly!" she said ecstatically. "Isn't it beautiful? Don't you just *love* the first snow of the year?" Kate hugged me, sharing her joy.

I hugged her back because I like Kate, but I detest snow. In fact, I detest winter.

Kate and Henderson and Stein and Ayers began rolling a snowman. We live in a northern New Hampshire town renowned for three things: a men's college, a ski slope, and the annual Ice Sculpture Festival. In other towns, you might not see too many high school seniors making snow people all over the place. In this town, it's practically a federally mandated activity.

Kate actually took off her mittens to use her bare hands for molding a few snowy features. Henderson gave the snow person a pony-tail — you have to be a real snow expert to do that! — and Ayers began pressing its upper regions to give it a Miss America figure. It made my whole body ache with cold just thinking about snow on that part of my anatomy.

I stepped back slightly so I could stand behind Jamie Winter — I couldn't imagine having to say that word all year round — but his shoulders did not have any particular effect at blocking the horrid, biting wind. He was wearing earmuffs, a form of protection I have always found useless, and his thick blond hair blew over and around the muffs, dancing in the wind. I have long brown hair, and I rarely wear it down. If it blows in the wind, it gets in my mouth and my eyes.

The school bus was late.

"I've decided what I'm going to do when I graduate," said Kate. Miraculously, she did not slip any snowballs or ice packs down my back. Turning seventeen had done wonderful things for Kate's behavior.

"I thought you decided last week to write advertising slogans," I said.

"That was last week. Saturday I was buying a new lipstick and I changed my mind. I'm going to be a New Lipstick Namer." Kate dug her new lipstick out of her purse and showed it to me. "My lipsticks will be named Cinnamon Snowhaze. Frozen Plum Wine. Icicle Peach."

Even the lipsticks around here are wintry, I thought. "I happen to own Cinnamon Snowhaze," I said. "That one's taken."

"That's not what you're wearing, is it?" said Kate, peering at my mouth.

"I'm wearing Chap Stick," I said, "so that I can keep my lips in working order."

Jamie and I grinned spontaneously at each other, as if we were both active in the Chap Stick industry, and I thought what a nice smile Jamie had. It understood me completely.

"You should put lipgloss over your Chap Stick," said Kate. "To get color."

She had a point. Since my blood had ceased

to circulate on exposed areas like my face, I needed some false coloring there.

"How do you like Burgundy Chill?" said Kate. "Or Wine Glacier?"

Jamie had been listening with interest. "You should be honest when you name them," he said firmly. "I suggest Isopropyl Lanolate. Or Microcrystalline Wax."

I laughed, and he chuckled and shook his head and the sandy hair fell in new patterns. I couldn't decide if Jamie needed a haircut or not. It was such nice hair, it would be a shame to discard any of it. His cheeks were ruddy from the cold, as though someone wearing Burgundy Chill lipstick had kissed him a hundred times. His golden hair framed that face perfectly.

"Somehow," said Kate, "Microcrystalline Wax lacks rhythm."

The bus finally arrived, its exhaust hanging in the air like a dragon's breath. I clambered on, my poor frozen joints creaking. Technically the bus has a heater. Factually, however, the heat is generated by forty high-school bodies. I personally could not afford to lose any more body heat. But at least being on the bus was an improvement over having my feet on solid ice.

"What do you want for Christmas?" said Kate dreamily.

"Christmas! Kate, we've hardly finished up Halloween!"

"Snow makes me think of Christmas. Gosh, last year we didn't get snow till January. Remember how crummy last year was?" she said, clearly still grieving for those snowless months. "And look at this, Holly! November tenth and we've got six inches of snow. It's going to be a wonderful, *wonderful* year, Holly. I can feel it in my bones."

What I could feel in *my* bones was frozen marrow.

"I think I'd like a goose down comforter," said Kate. "Or an Atari video game for snowless days. Or a one-year ski lift pass." Kate stared dreamily at the roof of the bus. "What do you want for Christmas, Holl?" she said.

"Acapulco," I told her. I looked out the bus window. Winter's color is gray. Gray sky, gray clouds, gray streets and buildings. The only relief is the white snow and the black tree branches. I've read descriptions of our town, which is considered one of the most beautiful in New England. "Especially worth a visit in winter," say the guidebooks, "when the exquisite village green is frosted with snow and the church spires rise against a pure blue sky. The campus, with its lovely gothic buildings and endless holly hedges, presents a view far too beautiful to miss."

I disagree. What would be beautiful in winter would be Barbados. Or Bermuda.

"Hot in here," complained Henderson. He zipped off the sleeves of his ski jacket and sat there with his arms covered by nothing but thin oxford cloth.

I, too, have a sleeve-zipped ski jacket. I think by now the zippers have probably rusted together. My elbows get chilled easily.

I would like to live where I'm overdressed in a bikini. Where snow is something so unknown that school teachers have to use filmstrips to prove to doubting little kiddies that such a thing actually exists. Where the schools have water polo teams instead of ice hockey.

I go on these hot-climate fantasy jags.

Last year this time I was on a Hawaiian kick. I was planning to go to the University of Hawaii. I had the college catalog and everything in the library about Hawaii and everything their State Tourism Department would send me free.

By January I'd read everything I could find on Hawaii, and I switched to the Florida Keys. That entertained me until March. You'd think March would include a sign or two of spring, but no. March last year — compensating for Kate's crummy November and December — included seventeen inches of snow. I shovelled our front walk yet again, returned my Florida books to the library, and came home with an armload of books on Mexico.

Last week in English we had to write extemporaneous paragraphs. Mrs. Audette gave us three subject choices. The first was, What Did We Do All Summer? (I discarded that. All I did all summer was watch the gypsy moths eat the leaves from our trees, and that's something better forgotten than written about.) The second choice was, Eating Breakfast Out. I had to discard that, too. My parents don't let us eat breakfast out. They feel it's decadent. How can you thank God for McDonald's hotcakes? they want to know. *I* could thank Him just fine, being a fast-food junkie from way back, but I rarely get the chance. So I took choice three, What Do I Plan to Do with My Life?

Now, a girl whose father is a minister and whose mother is a college professor should surely have some impressive plans for her life, right? She should be marshaling her abilities, analyzing her options, and preparing her attack on the future. Considering careers and professions, discarding those that do not perfectly meet her assets and goals.

That's what you think.

That's also what my parents think, but right now I won't get into the various ways in which I have disappointed them.

"I'm going to get warm," I wrote for Mrs. Audette. "I shall begin by drifting south. When I reach a state of constant perspiration, I'll be south enough. Once the icebergs in my bloodstream have thawed out, I'll lift my previously frozen eyelids and look around at the palm trees and the blistering sun and figure out how to earn a living."

I got an A. It turned out that poor old Mrs. Audette is from Mississippi, and she's here only because her husband is a ski freak and not because she likes it.

My parents, however, were not thrilled by my little essay. "We've instilled our values in you!" they cried. "Pressed our hopes upon you, taught you what discipline and truth are — and *this* is what you yearn for? Hot weather?"

I appeased my father by saying maybe I would be a missionary in Africa, but he was suspicious of my motives. "God doesn't want people to be missionaries in Nigeria just because they got cold in New Hampshire," he said severely.

My parents have always worried that I would turn out to be an unstable link in the great chain of society . . . a rip in the fabric of humanity. Now that they had my essay in hand, their suspicions were confirmed.

My mother believes in dealing with problems from the most basic, unarguable positions. Toss out those college catalogs from Georgia, Florida, Arizona, and Hawaii, she said. Too far away and too expensive. You're going to the University of New Hampshire where you can go cheaply.

I said that in cold weather I didn't get enough red blood up to my brain for proper intake of knowledge, and my father said he'd had just about enough of my so-called sense of humor and we weren't discussing weather one more time this winter.

So here we were, in my eighteenth year, a third of the way into November, and my parents were eyeing me sadly and nervously because they were afraid they had failed. It was almost enough to make me want to stay out in the snow, away from their accusing looks.

I sneezed.

"Bless you!" said Kate.

I sneezed again. I wondered if I could transform two sneezes into impending pneumonia and be able to stay home and watch soap operas. Probably not. My parents are very dubious about claims to sickness. Any child who is not running a fever of one hundred and three is probably making it up.

In front of me, Henderson and Jesperson sat pummeling and jabbing each other the way boys do and talking about the joys of cross-country skiing and whether or not our team could win the championship. Kate had a ski gear catalog open to show me the fantastic, unbelievable pair of boots she was praying her parents would buy her for Christmas.

If my father caught me praying for material goods, he'd flip. "I wish I had a father who ran a fried chicken franchise," I said.

Kate gave me a peculiar look. "I didn't know you liked fried chicken that much," she said.

"I don't." It was impossible to explain.

"You still haven't told me what you want for Christmas," she said.

Bermuda? I thought. Straight A's? A scholarship to a hot-climate college? A boyfriend? A parent who did not embarrass me by praying in public every time two or three people stood in a cluster?

I settled on two gifts. A boy. In Bermuda. Perfect combination.

The bus stopped, and we were at school. Not a perfect combination this year. Not for me, at least. I don't think my life has ever been less perfect. The truth is, this year I hate school. I would have preferred to graduate last year. I feel too old for high school. I don't know if I've matured more or if the cold weather has prematurely aged me or if I'm just bored silly. Whatever it is, since school started September fifth, I have not felt a part of anything. I seem to be just going through the motions.

Or it may just be that every day starts out with homeroom, and homeroom is so ghastly it taints my entire morning. When your morning is shot, it tends to spoil the afternoon as well.

You see, this year there are fourteen more students in the high school than the building was intended to accommodate. I am told that the administration gave considerable thought to the problem of what to do with the extra fourteen when assigning homeroom, that one time of the day when all 846 of us have to sit down at the same time.

Well, 832 kids got classrooms with neat stuff like windows, blackboards, chairs, and clocks.

Fourteen of us got assigned to the basement.

Last year, there was this ugly little hole in the wall down in the basement that was used to store gymnastics mats and vaulting horses. This year, the ugly little hole in the wall stores us.

Every morning when I walk into that place, I feel like a convict up for a twenty-year stretch. Gray linoleum floors. Gray cement-block walls. Bare bulbs hanging from a gray, water-stained ceiling.

Once — only once — I complained to my father.

"Holly," he said. (He was fresh from a minister's conference on Hunger Throughout the World, and I should have known better.) "In Latin America, the average length of schooling is 1.9 years. In Bangladesh, they use pieces of cardboard for blankets. In Guatemala, some of the Indians live in huts made of cornstalks."

"It's a beautiful homeroom," I told him. "I love it."

It's hard to complain in my house.

Once when I was fed up with cafeteria food and sick of making sandwiches to carry, I complained. My father said that the number of people suffering from severe malnutrition in the world is estimated at 500 million and to eat my peanut butter-and-jelly sandwich and like it.

So I eat my peanut butter-and-jelly sandwich and like it, but nevertheless, in a very private complaint not to be forwarded to my father, school this year is *lousy*.

Starting with homeroom.

Now, my father feels I should never even *think* a thing like this, let alone *say* it, because every person on earth has fine qualities and we must love our neighbors, but the fact is that I am the only decent person in that homeroom. It's true. The other thirteen are complete and total duds.

There's Ted Zaweicki. A fat old thing with a brain like the rest of his lard. Impenetrable.

And Ron White, whose personal habits are so awful that when I listed them for my mother she said I had a disgusting imagination.

And Pete Stein, who is a winter sports freak and can't utter a complete sentence without the word *snow*. He just sits there massaging his muscles and talking about whether synthetics or wools keep your legs warmer.

("Now wait a minute," said Kate. "You can't say a homeroom with Pete Stein in it is nothing but duds. Pete Stein is wonderful. You even voted for him for class president." This was true. I also thought he made a fine goalie for the hockey team, and I had admired through the years all the many cups and trophies Stein had won. I liked him in the way one likes a huge, bumbling mongrel the neighbors own. But Stein was an athlete. A fine breed, excellent for TV entertainment on slow Sunday afternoons, but not the sort with whom I wish to strike up intimate friendships.)

The only other girl in the homeroom is Hope Martin. Hope is constructed on the cigarette principle: thin, sleek, and dangerous to my health. Hope has a designer label attached to everything she wears, carries, or smells of. Since my father does not allow designer labels in our house ("If God had meant for your jeans to have somebody else's name on them . . ."), I never know for sure whether I'm envious of Hope's labels or if I despise them. At least I always have something to read in homeroom.

"Have any dates this weekend, Hollyberry?" said Hope. She knew perfectly well I had not, and she just wanted to expose this fact to the rest of the homeroom. She used my nickname in the most offensive, provoking way possible.

"No," I said. "I studied my Spanish." The one subject in which I always get 100 is Spanish. It's because I'm very highly motivated. I figure when I move to that hot climate, Spanish will be extremely useful.

Hope chose to ignore the remark about my Spanish and went back to the topic of dates. "I did," she said, and she told us about them. Hope used to refer to her male admirers as if a pocket calculator could not possibly keep track of them all, but now she is dating a college junior and has discarded all the children with whom she used to associate. "Grey," said Hope, repeating his name lovingly. I don't know whether Grey is his first name or his last or whether the man has only one, and I refuse to exhibit any interest in him, so probably I'll never know. "Doesn't it sound suave and well-bred?" said Hope. "So adult. Just like Grey himself."

You can see that dating a college man has not done a lot for Hope's basic personality. Now she walks into high school as if she's just visiting, especially in this homeroom of rejects. By now the only thing the rest of us hope when listening to her is that she'll go away.

Saying "Hollyberry" had sparked the class's attention. My name has been the focus of jokes since nursery school. A minister's daughter named Holly Carroll should expect that kind of thing — Christmas Carol, Hymnbook Hannah, and Hollyberry are among the nicer variations I have endured. Everybody but the clods in this homeroom got bored with name-teasing me years ago; here, it's still a major source of entertainment.

"Hey," said Zaweicki, "you know, if Hollyberry married Vice-President Bush, she'd be Hollybushberry."

"True," said Ron White. "But if Holly married Dickie Wood," he added, referring to a freshman, "she'd be Hollywood."

You see why I feel older than my classmates? I was listening to that kind of stuff in the fifth grade, and they're still dishing it out. Unfortunately, I'm still reacting to it the way I did in the fifth grade: with a great deal of tension. My cheeks blazed red. I felt like a toaster with little hot wires on my face.

"Look at those cheeks!" yelled Zaweicki. "Now she's Holly *Blush* Berry!"

I would have liked to flatten Zaweicki's face with my Spanish book, but having tried the violence technique in the past, I know that a) I will owe a fine for damaging the book, and b) I will get teased for being the minister's daughter — "What would your father say to such an act of total aggression?" Zaweicki would demand.

I let the teasing drift over me. It was like letting a blizzard drift over me. Not too successful.

"She's trying to ignore us," said Ron White, "but it'll never work."

Hope sat calmly doing her nails. Nobody ever teases Hope. I don't know why.

Stein said, "You are *boring*, Zaweicki. *Shut up*, White."

They shut up instantly and even looked embarrassed. Stein is such a leader type that any side he's on is the winning side. "Thanks, Pete," I said.

He nodded, looking put upon, as though girls were always placing demands upon him and it was really irritating, sapping the energy he needed for winning hockey games and scholarships.

Finally the homeroom bell rang, and we chugged up the stairs out of the bowels of the basement and on to our first period classes.

Hope glided up the stairs just in front of me, and I read her jeans labels for two flights. If I did have labels on my clothes, I thought, mine would probably read "Irregulars and Seconds."

Between fourth and fifth period, Kate stopped me in the hall. "Lydia and I are going to go hunt for some good buys in secondhand ski boots," she said. "The fraternities over at the college are having a sale. You want to come? Anyhow," she added, grinning eagerly, "we might meet somebody interesting."

The odds were slim that tiny-footed Kate was going to find a good fit in a ski boot that a twenty-year-old male athlete could no longer wear. It was just an excuse to go over to the fraternity and check out the boys there. Now, I am always ready to meet interesting boys. The trouble is that a boy selling used ski boots is a boy looking for a new pair of ski boots, and therefore *not* a boy I would find interesting. I would be interested in the boys who were *not* thinking about skiing, and they wouldn't be at the sale, so what was the point in going, right?

Kate said, "It's only eleven degrees out, Holl. Wear your gloves."

Eleven degrees. In November. It was going to be one frigid winter.

Jamie Winter walked by, grinning at me. "Some expression on your face," he said. "All I have to do is look at you, Holly, and I can tell it's Monday, and snowing, and winter, and school."

I laughed, but nobody else seemed to get the joke.

Hope, standing behind me, said, "Honestly, Holly, with your looks you could be dating college boys, too. But no, you exchange jokes with Jamie. He's not even a senior, Holly. He isn't even *seventeen* yet!"

Hope was like wall-to-wall carpeting. Impossible to get away from. I wished she would roll up and go away.

"He's so *young*," said Hope. "Why even bother with him?"

"I'm not bothering with him," I snapped at her. "We just talked for twenty seconds, is that a crime?" Jamie was already turning the corner in the hallway. I hoped he had not heard Hope's remarks. He would think I was interested in him, that Hope and I had had some prior conversation about him. I wasn't interested in anybody, and certainly not sixteen-year-olds. Every male in the whole high school seemed too young to me. That was half my problem. I just couldn't seem to work up any enthusiasm for anybody this year.

I left Hope still expounding on the virtues of dating older men like her wonderful, suave Grey and went on to English. We were reading Dickens. Mrs. Audette was having us look at a particularly horrid chapter where the poor little urchin was shuddering with cold and neglect, and you could almost *feel* those chilblains on your icy little hands.

"What's a chilblain?" said Kate.

"A sore on your hands from too much exposure to cold," said Mrs. Audette.

O Hawaii. O Mexico, I thought. Save a corner for me! Before I get chilblains!

Two

When you live in a town like this, either you ski and skate and snowmobile, or you live like a hermit.

I go in stages.

Some weeks, I want company so much I go right out and face the ice and snow, pretending that I actually like that kind of thing. I've always *wanted* to lose my toes to frostbite. I *prefer* tears of wind-driven agony to tears over soap operas. I *like* using one Chap Stick per week keeping my lips from cracking open.

Other weeks I feel that everybody out there but me is insane. Who needs that kind of company? So unless I can manage the indoors angle of the outdoor sport (like sipping hot chocolate in the little muffin shop beside the skating pond, or eating popcorn in front of the fireplace at the ski lift shelter) I just stay home.

Now, at home I have three activities other than homework and chores, which I regard as burdens, not activities.

The first is reruns. I love television reruns. It's so comforting to see the same show you've already watched four times. I even watch "I Love Lucy" shows that were reruns when my *mother* was watching television. I like the ones where the heroines are always getting into embarrassing and stupid positions but somehow survive, like "The Mary Tyler Moore Show" or "Rhoda" or "LaVerne and Shirley." I can really identify with doing something stupid and having to pay for it.

If my parents are in a strict mood, which is often, and they are afraid all this television will destroy my moral fiber, I move into my second hobby, which is daydreaming.

I have never heard anybody mention this as a hobby, and I'm not sure why. Perhaps I'm the only one who does so much of it. Or maybe other people won't admit they like to sit around daydreaming. I daydream best when I'm doing something where nobody will interrupt me. Ironing, say. There is no way my mother is going to interfere when I voluntarily approach the ironing basket and get to work. It is possible to stare down into the pattern of a wrinkled shirt for fifteen minutes and still look occupied.

In my daydreams I am always slender and beautiful, cavity-free and complexion-perfect. I am someplace hot and exotic, preferably sandy, and I am resting up after doing something impressive and strenuous.

Now if my *mother* were having the daydream, it would be about the strenuous and impressive deed instead of the vacation afterward. No wonder my parents think I am basically lazy.

There is only one thing I do in life that requires effort. That's my dollhouse. I work on it in secret because I feel sort of funny about it. Kate knows, and Lydia, but I don't think anybody else does, and I'm not sure Kate and Lydia have the slightest idea how much time I spend on it.

My father built it for me years ago; I think I was five. It's an enormous Victorian dollhouse with nine rooms, and it has a wraparound porch with gingerbread trim, an attic, and a marvelous stairway that sweeps up through two curved landings.

When I first saw the dollhouse, I was totally uninterested. My father's heart was broken. Here he'd spent a thousand hours creating this work of art and all his little girl said was, "Didn't you get me anything else?"

Once in a while I'd arrange the dolls in different beds, or put the kitchen furniture up in the attic, or see if my plastic horses could gallop in the door, but that was the extent of it. It was last winter when I got interested again. I happened to notice that three of the rooms in the dollhouse were not furnished. You would think a girl as swift as I would have spotted this sometime during the previous decade, but as I said, the dollhouse was not my first concern during those years. Anyhow, I decided that given a choice between sledding with Kate or furnishing the library (I knew it was a library because my father had put a tiny brass plaque over the door that read SSSHHH!!! LIBRARY!!!), I would furnish the library.

I made shelving out of popsicle sticks that I stained brown with Magic Markers. I turned a macaroni box into an old scarred desk, covering it with brown paper and covering the brown paper with tiny graffiti. With a little bit of glue and gray satin, a plastic spool of thread became a shiny office chair. Books appeared from tiny squares of cardboard and wrapping paper.

Frankly, it was tacky looking. But it was such fun. I loved doing it. I loved those tiny little pieces and the steady wrist I needed and the teeny speck of glue it took, and the patience.

My parents had very mixed feelings. My mother worried that I was regressing. That I felt doomed to a lack of popularity and so retreated to my girlhood bedroom and occupied myself with babyish things. "Don't you want to be out with your friends?" Mother would say. And then, *very* understandingly, "Or did they go off without you? That's rough, isn't it, Holly? But I know how you feel, dear."

"Mother, Lydia and Kate and for that matter everybody else would be perfectly happy to have me meet them at the pond and skate."

"I'll buy you new skates. Your old ones probably squash your toes."

"No, thanks, Mom. Having old, crummy skates is a terrific excuse. I don't want to skate."

Then my father's even more mixed feelings would surface. On the one hand, he was darn glad that his gift of love and craft had been noticed after all these years. On the other hand, he worried that it wasn't normal to play with a dollhouse at my age. "It isn't good to isolate yourself from your fellow man," he would say nervously. "You need to join things, Holly. Be with your friends."

"Dad, I've been in school with them for seven hours today already. Isolated I'm not."

They were relieved to find magazines for adults printed to reach the miniatures enthusiast. When there was a dollhouse exhibit to raise money for playground equipment, they were even more relieved to find civilized, church-going adults participating in this sort of thing. And when the senior deacon of the church and his wife showed off *their* miniatures collections, my parents surrendered completely.

One day my father was watching me hack at bits of old balsa-wood flying airplanes, using a kitchen knife in an attempt to cut cradle pieces, and he said, "You're not using proper tools, Holly. Come on down to my workshop, and I'll teach you how to work with wood. Those flimsy little things you're making won't last long."

It was a whole new world. A world of tiny screwdrivers and miniature files, of tweezers and vises for making tiny furniture. It wasn't the world I'd been daydreaming about — that hot, sunny, sandy world — but it certainly kept me occupied through a long and frigid spring.

Even my mother got into the act. She loves needlework. To my complete surprise, she made a pair of tiny quilts for the twin beds in the dollhouse guest room, the smallest imaginable squares making the patterns.

When summer came — in northern New Hampshire it doesn't come for long — we went on long drives down unknown roads that wound through the patchwork quilt of forest and stone walls of rural New England. And what should we find in one village but a little shop that sold nothing but dollhouses and miniatures and dollhouse furniture kits. When we got over our total and absolute shock at the prices of those lovely Queen Anne hunt boards designed for a three-inch doll to serve from, we drove shakily on home.

Every Christmas my grandmother sends me a check. This year I was trying to decide whether to save it for my hot climate escape hatch fund, or buy a six-inch-tall clock that actually chimes and tells the time and wall sconces that actually have electrical connections.

Sometimes when I'm pouring over a catalog for dollhouse things I want the pieces so much I actually ache for them. Especially on Sundays it's hard to look at that dollhouse without a twinge of guilt. My father likes to tell me that there are places in, say, Brazil where half the children die before age one because they have no milk and perhaps no safe water. Instead of sending my grandmother's Christmas check to them, or at the very least planning on how I'm going to save the world, I sit and daydream about buying a miniature fireplace screen, or plan decorating the dollhouse parlor for Christmas.

Sometimes I wonder if my father goes through life feeling guilty, or if being a minister sort of takes the edge off.

I could ask him, of course, and he'd love it, but the trouble is that Dad answers things too thoroughly. When I'd like a two sentence answer, I get a two-hour sermon.

My current project for the dollhouse is a Christmas tree. I cut it from balsa, slotting three tree shapes together to make a six-winged tree, and now the green paint I'd sprayed on was dry so I could paint the bells and candles and tinsel and popcorn. Now, painting those tiny, tiny decorations takes a steady hand, believe me.

The phone rang, taking my mind off my guilt. It was Kate. Kate is sunshine. If she's ever had a doubt or a fear, she's never mentioned it in my presence. "Holly!" she said, bubbling even more than usual. "You'll never guess what!"

"What?"

Kate paused for a moment so I could sense that it really was something special. Finally she said, "Gary Beaulieu asked me out on Friday!"

"Oh, Kate!" I said, delighted for her. Gary was a really nice guy. As far as I knew, he'd never asked a girl out except to the occasional class dances, and he'd never asked the same girl twice. He was much too athletic and winter sports oriented for me — a sidekick of Pete Stein — and yet curiously enough I felt a little pang of unhappiness at the thought of Kate going out with him. Once again, it was somebody else dating, and not me. "That's super, Kate!" I said. "He's a doll."

My dolls were three inches high. Hers were living, breathing six-foot males.

Kate talked happily about the date they would have Friday. *I'm not jealous*, I told myself.

"There's one problem, Hollyberry," said Kate anxiously.

"What's wrong?"

"I have to babysit Friday," she said. "I agreed ages ago. Do you think you could sit for me?"

"Oh, Kate, you know I would, but I'm already sitting. Mr. and Mrs. Dallimonti."

"Oh, no!" said Kate, almost in tears. "I was sure you'd be able to help me. Can you think of anybody else I could call? I already accepted the date because I was so sure I could find someone."

"Lynn Vining?" I said. "Or Sally? Or maybe Gretchen?"

My father yelled from downstairs. "Holly! Don't stay on the phone so long! I want the line open!"

He always wants the line open. He's convinced that some suicidal parishioner will try to call just when I'm using the phone to talk about hair styles or something. There's never been a suicidal parishioner in his church that I know of, but he really has a thing about keeping the phone line free. I can never talk more than fifteen minutes.

"I know, I know," said Kate glumly.

We were silent for a moment, thinking. Of course, Kate could always back out of her babysitting job, but then she'd feel so guilty all Friday night she couldn't enjoy herself with Gary. "Listen, Kate," I said. "The Dallimontis have only the one little girl, and Nancy is seven, after all, and absolutely no problem. Who are you sitting for? Could I combine kids in one house?"

I could almost feel Kate hugging me. "Oh, Hollyberry, I love you. It's the Smith baby. I bet you could. Mrs. Smith and Mrs. Dallimonti wouldn't mind."

I said I'd call them both and be sure.

Kate said I was the most terrific person she knew.

It wasn't in quite the same league with feeding the starving in Bangladesh, but it certainly did make me feel better. I made a miniature Christmas present for my dollhouse tree and tied the silver embroidery thread bow with pleasure.

Three

It was a few weeks after the double babysitting job that Christopher asked if he could practice on me.

He came into my bedroom at about ten at night and just sat on the edge of the mattress and looked at me nervously. "Did you break something?" I said. "You look as if you hope Mom and Dad won't get home for two years."

Christopher tried to laugh. Instead, he just looked pinched around the mouth. Whatever he'd done, it must be pretty awful.

It's strange to watch a kid brother grow up. For years and years, Christopher was nothing but a shrimp, a loud-mouthed pest. I steered around him, speaking only if absolutely necessary. Christopher always had sand in his shoes and peanut butter in his hair and D's on his report card.

Then all of a sudden — wham!

There was this six-foot-tall, handsome man living in my house — and it was my little brother.

I don't even feel acquainted with the present Christopher. He's so different from the shrimpy pest of the past that I sometimes think a substitution was worked when I wasn't looking. "What's your problem, Christopher?" I said.

It's never wise to ask Christopher that. While I loathe telling anybody my problems, Christopher loves to. He'll tell Dad for an hour and Dad will give him support and feedback, being a minister experienced in comfort sessions. Then Christopher'll tell Mother for an hour, and she'll give him insight and understanding, being a college prof accustomed to young people with difficulties. Yuck.

But Christopher, to my surprise, did not settle down on my bed, close up my chemistry book for me, and start in on a long monologue about how life is hard and nobody cares enough. He said, "Holly, if I put some music on, would you dance with me?"

My lower half slid off the bed, partly due to Christopher's weighing it down and creating a path and partly due to sheer astonishment. "Dance with you?" I said.

He looked down at the rug, over at the wall, and finally into the dollhouse, where he seemed deeply interested in the miniature bookshelf. "Yeah," he said.

Christopher was not a dancer. Christopher could hardly *count* to four in rhythm, let alone dance. "Why?" I said suspiciously.

"Because I'm taking Alison Coffey out tomorrow night to the junior class dance, and I need the practice."

My little brother.

First I babysat so Kate could have a date. Now I was to be dance instructor so my little brother could have a date. I was sitting around doing homework and thinking about miniature furniture and daydreaming of hot climates, and here was my kid brother getting on with life and asking girls to dances.

I wrote another three numbers down in my chemistry calculations. They were wrong and I'd have to erase them, but it gave me something to do. My stomach hurt a little.

"You don't have to," said Christopher, flushed with embarrassment. He got up off the bed.

"Sure," I told him. "Glad to."

The saint in action, I thought to myself. I

may never have a social life of my own, but at least I'll be known far and wide for my generosity and overwhelming kindness.

Christopher slid a cassette into his cassette player, put the volume on high, and gave me a fierce and sudden hug. At first I was kind of tickled to have all that brotherly affection and then I realized he was dancing with me. "Maybe a little looser," I said. "Think how annoyed Mrs. Coffey would be if you suffocated Alison on the very first date."

"Very funny," said Christopher. But he held me looser.

I am a pretty good dancer. It's too bad I have no one to dance with these days except myself or my brother. I debated what a saint would say in these circumstances. "Actually, Christopher," I told him, "you're not too bad."

Christopher smiled complacently.

I said, "You don't need that much practice. You're fine. Alison is going to have a ball."

Christopher swaggered around the bedroom, agreeing with me.

"You want to rehearse something to talk about?" I said. "That could be a problem."

"Heck, no. I never have any problem talking to Al Coffey. In fact, I have a problem finding empty air time to fit my words in. The only human being on earth who talks more than Al is her mother."

I got bored being saintly. "Give Al a few years," I predicted. "She's going to surpass Mrs. Coffey before long."

Christopher just grinned, as if he'd considered the possibility of himself and Alison aging together, and I had a sudden lurch of the brain, feeling younger than my brother. Feeling awkward and gawky and little. Gosh, I thought, is he just sixteen? He seems so old, suddenly. And I seem so *young*.

I sank back down and stared glumly at my chemistry. I like to finish my homework on Friday nights. Otherwise it just seems to lurk there all weekend, like Evil, hunkering around Sunday evening and ruining it.

"Mind rehearsing something else?" said Christopher.

His anxiety was back. He was fidgeting and tugging at his belt loops. He looked like a very tall first-grader. I liked him much better when I was older and calmer and he was younger and more worried. "What else is there?" I said. I definitely was not going to rehearse kissing.

"The car." Christopher got his driver's license last month. It occurred to me that part of the reason he wanted to date was that he needed somebody to show off his driving skills to. The rest of us just weren't very impressed.

"I want to practice putting a girl in and out of the car."

"You make it sound like a box for United Parcel. Anyway, Alison may be the self-reliant type, and she'll get in and out of the car herself."

"Just in case," said Christopher. "Please? Be helpful and useful, please?"

How repellent, I thought. Here I am, aching to be slinky, alluring, sexy, and breathtaking, and what does he call me? Helpful and useful. Sainthood is a drag.

"I also want to practice holding your coat up for you so I get your hand started in the armholes right."

I wondered if somewhere out there, beyond the drifts of snow and the glossy sheets of ice, there was a boy rehearsing how to put a coat on *me*. Stranger things have happened, I told myself.

I lapsed into a little daydream, where this suave gentleman helped me in and out of fur coats and cranberry-red Mercedes.

"Please?" said Christopher.

He has huge brown eyes. When he was small, people used to exclaim over him and claim to be absolutely melting under that gaze. When he was a grubby little urchin growing up, the effect of the eyes was lost in the general filth and hanging hair, but now the eyes had it again. Christopher turned them on me, as though he were some superhero, and tried to melt me.

"Okay, okay," I said. I wondered how Alison Coffey felt when he tried his eye-melting technique on her. I wondered when I was going to melt somebody with *my* eyes.

They'd probably think my mascara was blinding me and hand me a Kleenex. Besides, I didn't know who I'd want to melt in the first place.

So we practiced. We got in and out of my coat at least twenty times, with Christopher demanding me to be more awkward so he could be prepared for Alison's worst. Then we practiced getting in and out of the car, so Christopher wouldn't slam any doors on Al's feet or scarf tips.

"You were wonderful, Christopher," I said at last, heading back into the house. "I wouldn't sit in a freezing car on a freezing night for just anybody. But now we know that you can open doors with the best of them."

Christopher beamed at me and loped on into the house. A little of his polish dimmed: He forgot to hold the door open for me. By the time I got there, it had slammed and locked. I rang the doorbell for about ten minutes before he came back to let me in.

"What took you so long?" I yelled. "It'll

take me half the night to thaw out! I probably have frostbite! I bet I rang that bell for thirty minutes!"

"Long!" yelped Christopher. "It took me about fifteen seconds."

"I almost died out there. Do you have any idea what the windchill factor is right now?" I demanded.

Christopher just looked at me, and I had the same lurching, unpleasant feeling of being the younger one. The shrimp and the pest. "Honestly, Holly," he said, sighing in annoyance, "people get tired of you always knocking the weather. It's boring. Everybody loves winter. No wonder you don't have any dates. Every time a guy is good at something, like ice hockey or cross-country, you make some snide remark about your blood congealing."

He went up the stairs three at a time, and I didn't even have the front door properly closed by the time he was dialing the upstairs telephone. "Hello, Al?" he said eagerly. "How're you doing?"

I leaned against the door, feeling a draft, feeling lonely and worthless. I will not cry, I said to myself. It is all right for me to dislike winter. Weather does not completely dominate my thoughts. I don't go without dates just because I don't like winter. I go without dates because . . .

I found that I really did not want to consider why I went without dates. There are times when you are ready for heavy thinking and times when you are not. Instead I walked into the TV room and switched on the tube. You never have to think when you're watching television.

Seconds later my parents came in, moaning about how stupid the meeting had been and how stupid our elected officials were and how they didn't know why they were even bothering. I could identify with that. I moved over on the couch and my father flopped down beside me. We fought over who got most of the afghan. I won.

"What are you watching?" said Dad. "It can't be any more rotten than that shabby excuse for democracy we just came from."

"I just tuned in. It's a movie, but I don't know what."

We watched intently for about one minute, discovering nothing, and then a commercial came on. My father can't stand commercials. He likes us to talk through them. "Annie," he said to my mother, "please create a distraction. If I see one more Irishman pushing deodorant soap, I'm going to have a heart attack."

I found myself memorizing the commercial. Every time Dad makes us turn the sound down on an advertisement, I am seized by the overpowering desire to lip synch the words and sing lustily of American-made cars or tougher floor waxes.

The station identification came on. It was a five-second spot showing our village green, drenched in glittering snow, with the TV station letters seemingly impaled on the steeple of our church.

"Isn't that beautiful, Stewart?" said my mother in a dreamy voice. "Doesn't it restore your faith to see that, dear?"

My father didn't seem particularly restored, but he did kiss her.

"Somehow all that lovely pure white snow crusting the spire makes it all seem worthwhile," said my mother. "I don't think there's anything lovelier than our village in winter."

I reached for the *TV Guide*. I personally felt there was considerable room for improvement. Like a geographical position one thousand miles farther south and a lot of handsome, nonathletic seventeen-year-old boys.

F^{our}

A car went past us, flinging up white snow and turning it gray. I knew it was Ted Zaweicki, because he feels the entire *state* should listen to his radio. I'm surprised his car hasn't vibrated apart at the seams. "If Ted had heart failure, no one would ever know," I muttered.

I thought I was alone at the bus stop. Everybody else was in the field practicing. The Ice Sculpture Festival has lots of prizes; most inventive, most lifelike, largest, and so forth. If you win, you get lots and lots of attention and your picture in the paper and invitations to the Ice Ball and so on. I'd love to have all that without having to make an ice sculpture, but this seemed unlikely.

"That's true," said Jamie Winter. "His car would go right on making his heart fibrillate."

I had forgotten Jamie, leaning so silently on the phone pole beside me. We agreed that Zaweicki and his car were possibly the two least useful commodities in New Hampshire. The music in Zaweicki's wake was still hanging in the air, as if it had frozen there. I couldn't recognize the song. The volume completely distorted it.

"Those singers took voice lessons from a wolf," I said.

It wasn't my best line, but Jamie grinned. It was the kind of grin people give when you're not really a comedian but they like you, so they smile to keep your humor company.

It occurred to me that Jamie was very good-looking. This was not the first time I had made this observation, but it was the first time I'd actually thought about it at length. I had this terrible impulse to kiss him.

Oh, wow, I thought. He's sixteen. He's Christopher's age. That's when you know it's really a lousy winter. When you're ready to kiss little-brother types. "Who do you have in English Comp this year?" I said, to keep my lips moving and thus prevent them from freezing into an awkward expression.

Some poor little frostbitten dog skittered

across the road in front of us and just barely missed being hit by another car.

"Zinn," said Jamie. "We just had her usual 'What Do You Plan to Do in Life That Will Affect the World?' writing assignment."

"Oh, I remember it well! I wrote what I thought was a witty and brilliant one-word response."

"One *word*?" said Jamie. "For an essay? What was the word?"

"Survive."

Jamie laughed. "I can just imagine her reaction to *that*. 'One word, Miss Carroll, does not an essay make.' "

We giggled.

"What did you write?" I said to Jamie.

"Oh, the usual. First I plan on negotiating peace in the Middle East. Then I'm thinking of dabbling in silver futures for my first million dollars. Perhaps after that I'll salvage the *Titanic*, and of course before I'm thirty I plan to put an end to world famine."

"Did you get an F?" I said. "Zinn wants her assignments taken seriously." Together Jamie and I chirped Mrs. Zinn's favorite closing line. "*English*," we said, "is preparation for *life*, and *life* is not a *joke*."

"Holly, Holly," said Hope Martin, in her thick, lazy voice. She had just come to the bus stop. "In a town full of college men you keep going after high school juniors?" She looked at Jamie as if he were an eight-year-old with no front teeth and a collection of snails in his pockets.

"I'm not going after anybody, Hope," I said irritably, knowing even as I protested that I should have stayed silent, because Hope was always looking for a new teasing front, and Jamie might well supply her with one.

Hope had Grey with her. Grey was wearing a beautiful down-puffed jacket, slim cut, so he didn't look like a walking bathtub the way most people do in down coats. He even had the jacket unbuttoned. Now, I ask you, what is the point of buying a down coat to warm your body when you go and leave the coat unbuttoned?

Pencils were growing out of Grey's shirt pocket like a picket fence. I got the message. He was rich (the down jacket) and macho (the *open* down jacket) and athletic (the muscles under the open down jacket) and also a scholar (pencils).

Grey said, "Hope, I hate dumping you here like this."

"It's okay, love. You couldn't get the car started, that's all. I understand." She kissed him.

Getting a car going in subzero weather is no

easy trick. You need shelter, heaters, and a good measure of luck. College kids whose cars sit out on the mountainside often walk.

"No mechanical sense, huh, Grey?" said Jamie gladly.

Grey looked at Jamie without interest. "Who's that?" he said to Hope.

"Nobody," said Hope. "A kid. Sixteen."

They stood right there next to us and proceeded to discuss important things, like the fact that she could eat at his fraternity the following night and did she like fried apples?

"My *age* doesn't make me nobody," said Jamie. "My personality might. But merely being sixteen does not cancel my existence."

I saluted him, but neither Hope nor Grey even looked up.

Grey said, "I don't know about Saturday, Hope. I may have to skip the festivities then. I really do have to study now and then. How would you feel about skipping our date Saturday?"

Grey's voice was never-changing. Smooth, suave, one word never seeming to mean more than any other. Hope, however, was very dramatic. "Grey!" she said. "If you desert me on a Saturday night, I shall fling myself down the stairs!"

"You live in a ranch house, Hope," said Jamie.

I doubled over laughing, and Jamie and I whopped each other on the back, enjoying his joke. Hope looked at us in revulsion. "Grey, *please* get your car fixed. I hate riding on the bus with these kids. They're all so juvenile."

The bus arrived before Jamie could make another comment, and everybody else deserted his or her snow person to shove and elbow into the bus. In the thick of this press, Kate said to me, "Holly, if you're going to make an effort with a boy, why not Pete Stein? Why Jamie? He's only sixteen."

Jamie was already on the bus, making his way toward the rear where the sophomores and juniors sat. I said, "We were just talking, Kate. Is it a crime to laugh?"

"No, but Holl, it looks as if you stand there every day just so Jamie can stand there and talk with you. I mean, people are starting to wonder. You can't go out with a junior. Nobody does that."

"I'm not dating him," I protested. "I'm not thinking about dating him, either. I'm just standing there, and he's making funny remarks, and I'm laughing."

Obviously Kate thought I was weird. And Kate has to be the most open-minded person I know. If Kate thought I was weird, who knew what everybody else was thinking.

I sank back in my seat and told myself I

didn't care what everybody else thought; I was my father's daughter, and I could shrug off the comments of the world and take the path less traveled by . . . but it was not true. I didn't want them talking about me and making sideways faces at me and snickering. I didn't want to be different. It was different enough just to be Holly Carroll, minister's daughter, dollhouse-builder, and winter-hater.

"I mean, there are eleven hundred college men running around this town," said Kate. "You don't need to look at rejects like Jamie Winter."

"He isn't a reject," I said. "He's just *younger*."

Kate looked at me nervously, as though she was afraid I would next announce my engagement to this younger person. She began telling me about her date with Gary Beaulieu. I don't know if she was trying to change the subject or encourage me with descriptions of excellent eighteen-year-olds, but what she did was depress me terribly.

My pesky kid brother Christopher was dating. My best friend Kate was dating. My nemesis-in-homeroom Hope had dated since she was in her cradle. And what was I doing? Talking to some junior about English assignments.

We were passing Nelson's Clothiers on the

opposite side of College Avenue. There's a sign in the window at Nelson's: CLOSED FOR INVENTORY. The sign's been up for two years. They take very thorough inventories in Nelson's. "I am beginning to suspect," I told Kate, "that Nelson's has gone out of business, but I don't want to be premature in my judgment."

Kate giggled. "You're so funny, Holl," she said.

I was about to tell her that the person who was funny was Jamie Winter, but then I thought, better not. If I keep bringing him up, she'll start worrying about me. Pretty soon there'll be gossip about Jamie and Hollyberry. I'll be accused of cradle-robbing, and Jamie will get teased for wanting older women. And I'll be embarrassed because Jamie didn't mean a thing by it, and he'll be humiliated because everyone will think he did.

Life, I thought, staring at the fresh flakes of snow that were gently drifting down on the street and the cars, is too complex for me.

F^{ive}

"Oh, come on, Holly," said Lydia irritably. "Don't be such a spoilsport all the time. You won't go skating. You won't go skiing. Now you won't even go to the movies with us! I'm beginning to think that you have whatever it is, that fear of crowds, or something."

"Agoraphobia," said Kate. "She doesn't have agoraphobia, Lydia."

I shifted my weight from one frozen foot to the other. I know I spend the majority of my time comfortably indoors, but my winter memories are all of the *discomfort* outdoors. "Can't go," I said. I tried to think of good excuses other than the real one, but I am not much of a fibber. I'm not sure if it's lack of practice or the conscience my parents instilled in me, but I find fake excuses hard to come by.

"Look at it this way, Holly," said Kate. "The movie is inside. It's going to be hot in there. You can have buttered popcorn and chocolate-covered raisins. Not one single cold-weather worry."

I thought about having hot buttered popcorn in my left hand and chocolate-covered raisins in my right hand and a large soda propped between my knees. My brother thinks it's completely revolting to eat those three things at one time, but I think it's heaven. I'd be willing to watch anything in exchange for buttered popcorn and chocolate-covered raisins. I said, "But I can't."

Even Kate was exasperated with me. "Holly, none of us has a date for tonight. And it's a terrific movie. Everybody says so. The critics even say so. Even Mrs. Audette says so, and she thinks movies are an insult to the book. Come on."

I gave up trying to think of excuses. Miserably, I said, "My father won't let me go."

"Then we'll go tomorrow when you aren't busy with your father," said Lydia.

"She means her father the minister thinks there's too much sex and violence in the film, and she can't see that one at all," said Kate.

Kate heaved a sigh. She knows my father almost as well as I do. Maybe better; she still goes to the youth group meetings and I dropped out the day I turned sixteen. I always hated church activities, but my parents said I had to go till I was sixteen, and then I could make up my own mind. They probably figured by the mature age of sixteen I'd love it so much I'd want to run it myself. They were pretty upset when I said, "Well, that's it for church." But it was a promise, and they keep their promises, so they let me drop out. Not, I might add, without daily reminders that the church group still existed should I deign to appear.

Lydia said, "How's he going to know? Just tell your father we're going to play Monopoly at my house and how's he going to know we really went to the movies? Come on, Holly, that's no excuse. You'll love the flick, I know you will."

I thought about promises. I had not promised not to see the movie. But then, my father hadn't thought extracting a promise was necessary. He said not to go, therefore his daughter would not go.

"Don't be such a sheep, Holly," said Lydia. "Honestly, in some ways I feel so much older than you. Still scurrying around doing exactly what Mummie and Daddy say. Making eyes at sixteen-year-old boys, for heaven's sake. Playing with a dollhouse!"

She made me sound about twelve. I winced at the description.

"The movie isn't bad," said Kate. "My sister saw it. She said it was really funny and most of the violence was offstage and the sex was kind of sweet and tender. Not raunchy."

"Just don't tell your father," said Lydia. "What he doesn't know won't hurt him."

Everything hurts my father. Starving children in Africa, imprisoned people in America, young mothers dying of cancer, teenagers on drugs, and other people's marriages breaking up. My father is bruised and battered by the entire world.

Lydia was looking at me out of the corners of her eyes. She has slightly slanting eyes, as if mixed in with all her French and German and Scottish ancestry is one lone Oriental, and nobody can look more superior and more bored than Lydia. Not even Hope.

Lydia's writing me off, I thought. All my mother's predictions are going to come true. If I don't do this, I *will* be the one left out. The girl nobody invites to skating parties and never thinks of for gossip on the phone.

"Okay," I said. "I'll meet you at Kate's around six-thirty."

"Good," said Lydia. She patted me. Then

I really felt about twelve years old and part of the dollhouse set. Being *patted*.

All through the school day I stewed over my decision. First I'd feel guilty. Then I'd be mad at all my parents' archaic, unfair demands. Then I'd think, at least I ought to argue with my father first, tell him what I want, be up front about it instead of lying. Then I'd think, how can I be old enough to graduate from high school if I can't even choose my own entertainment?

I worried so much I forgot I had a bus to catch after school and by the time I remembered it, the bus was long gone. I was stranded three miles from home, and there were six inches of snow on the ground. Of course the sidewalks — where there were sidewalks — were salted and scraped, so that if I was lucky I'd hit only a few hundred patches of ice on which to slip. I am the sort of girl whose ankles automatically bend at the sight of ice and whose rear end can always find the deepest, wettest slush to fall in. I wondered what the odds were that the car that ran me down would have metal treads in its snow tires.

This kind of thing doesn't happen to a person in Hawaii, I thought sadly.

And on top of that, I'd left my scarf and mittens in my so-called homeroom.

"Hi, Holly," said a familiar voice. "Need a ride home?"

"Oh, Jamie! Were lovelier words ever uttered! Yes, I do." It was on the tip of my tongue to say, *I didn't know you could drive yet*, but I stopped myself in time. Fleetingly I thought of Lydia accusing me of making eyes at a sixteen-year-old. Well, Lydia wasn't here. As she liked to say, what she couldn't see wouldn't hurt her.

Jamie even took some of my books. That boy has possibilities, I thought to myself. "Jamie," I said, "could you possibly wait another moment while I race down to homeroom and get my scarf and mittens?"

"Sure. Where's your homeroom?"

"Mr. Tartrella. Basement detail."

"I've heard about that place. Never have seen it. Mind if I tag along?"

"Step right up. The chance of your life. See the famous quarantine room for the forgotten fourteen."

Jamie laughed. We clattered down the stairs together, Jamie wisecracking every step of the way. Mr. Tartrella was still in the room, gathering up his attendance and cafeteria papers. Mr. Tartrella is not known for his speedy achievement levels. He's in charge of our Educational Technology Department (known in my mother's day as Filmstrips). "Hello, Mr. Tartrella," I said.

He looked at me vaguely. After all, when you have all of fourteen kids in your home-room, and only two of them girls, it isn't easy to remember their names and faces. "Hunh?" he said nasally.

Jamie looked gravely at Mr. Tartrella, at the gray ceiling with its exposed bulbs, and at the torn leather on the vaulting horses where Stein and White usually perched. "Mr. Tartrella?" he said.

"Hunh?"

"Is this homeroom up to the standards man-dated by federal laws?"

I burst out laughing.

Mr. Tartrella said, "Hunh?"

I pulled my mittens on and tossed my scarf around my neck, and Jamie and I left the room. "Does he ever say anything besides *hunh*?" said Jamie.

I reflected. "Well, he's been known to say *naah* and *yup*," I told Jamie, "but not often enough to consider them parts of his working vocabulary."

Jamie's turn to double over laughing. He spilled my books all over the basement stairs. If I'd dumped the books, I would have been embarrassed and awkward, trying to gather them all up, and struggling to be graceful while doing it, but Jamie barely noticed. Still laugh-ing, he picked up the books almost as if he'd meant to drop them, and we walked up the stairs. "That homeroom," he said, "is about as attractive as the inside of a cereal box."

I hadn't done so much laughing in ages. I'd forgotten how wonderful it feels to have your cheeks bunch up from grinning, and your eyes crinkle with chuckling, and your whole body aching in a funny way with so much laughter.

"Who else is in that homeroom?" he said.

"*La crème de la crème*," I told him. "People like Ron White, Ted Zaweicki, Rich Ayers, Hope Martin."

We both groaned. It was as much fun groaning as laughing. Jamie opened the door of his car for me, and I thought of Christopher rehearsing and blushed. Jamie drove pretty well. I wondered how long he'd had his license. I liked watching his hands on the wheel. He had large hands, much larger than mine. I found myself wanting to hold them, curl his fingers around mine.

"What are you doing tonight?" said Jamie.

"Going to a movie with Kate and Lydia."

"Yeah? Which one?"

I told him. We were almost at my house. "I saw that movie," he said, sounding surprised. "I thought your father was pretty strict about stuff like that. Didn't he object to your seeing it? Or doesn't he know what it's about?"

I decided not to incriminate myself by answering that one. I said, "What did you like best about the movie, Jamie?"

"Leaving," he said firmly.

I laughed in spite of myself.

Christopher was sweeping snow off the steps, getting rid of the afternoon's flurries. He paused midsweep and stared at me getting out of Jamie Winter's car.

"Bye, Jamie," I said, slamming the door. "Thanks a lot."

"It was a pleasure," he said gravely.

I scurried up the sidewalk, and Christopher leaned on his broom and said, "Jamie *Winter*? Holly, he's *my* age. You're a *senior*. And he's a bore, besides."

"He is not boring," I said. "Anyhow, he just gave me a ride home." I thought of how I had wanted to hold Jamie's hand, and I flushed.

Nothing slips by Christopher. "What happened to the bus?" he said, eyeing my hot cheeks suspiciously.

"I missed it."

Christopher looked at me as if any fool knew that missing the bus was a ruse to get a ride home with Jamie. He said, "So old Holly's falling for Jamie Winter, huh? Can't you date someone your own age?"

"I'm not dating him!" I yelled. "I'm not

even *thinking* about him! I just took advantage of his car!"

"That's typical of girls. Girls are selfish, unpleasant, grabbing creeps. All you want is free rides and gasoline. Don't give a thing in return."

Snow has its uses. I dropped everything, made the quickest snowball in history, and got my worthless little brother right in the face. What do I mean — little? He's now six inches taller than I am. I have to throw uphill. I felt that I was defending old Alison's right to give nothing in return for free rides. Christopher and I had a snowball fight that threatened to be the death of us both, and I stopped only because I had a sudden thought, not related to Christopher or Alison or rides or snow.

Why had Jamie asked me what I was doing Friday night?

Six

I had plenty of time to wonder about Jamie.

On Sunday morning, Lydia's father told my father how nice it was that the girls had all gone to a movie together just like old times. My father said, "I thought they were going to play Monopoly." Lydia's father said, "They're too old for that, Stewart. Where'd you get an idea like that?"

Fortunately my father is nonviolent. All that happened was a sad lecture in how I disappointed his trust, and he grounded me for two weeks. *Very* grounded. No *nothing*.

I stared into the attic of my dollhouse and wondered if I should have a maid living up there. Decorate it in gray and white and black, appropriate for a girl in domestic service.

But I couldn't get interested.

"Kate's parents," I told my mother and father at supper, "don't care what she sees or what she reads. They believe she is sufficiently mature to sift the reasonable and the good from the unreasonable and the bad. They feel —"

"Holly," said my mother softly and with a lot of hostility, "I don't care in the slightest what Kate's parents feel about anything."

From the look in her eyes it was best to drop the topic and accept being grounded a little more gracefully.

I kept thinking about Jamie Winter.

Very nice person. Very good-looking. Very amusing. Definitely no more fond of frigid weather than I.

But try as I might, I could not manage a single romantic thought toward him. He was just sixteen years old. Christopher's age, for heaven's sake. Just some boy who stood around waiting for the same bus.

Perhaps he would be driving every day now, though, if his mother would let him use the car that often. Would I mind if he didn't stand with me and crack jokes while everybody else sculpted snow people? If he offered to drive me home every day, the way Grey drove Hope, would I accept?

That was a tough question. On climate

grounds, definitely I would accept a ride rather than endure the cold. On boyfriend grounds, that meant accepting the teasing and the funny looks from an entire school, and I doubted that Jamie's jokes, however amusing, were worth that.

I tried to come up with one boy — *any* boy — in the entire school over whom I could really flip. But everyone I could name had so many drawbacks. Perfection, I thought — is that an unreasonable thing to ask? Should I allow some ice-hockey jock to date me?

I laughed at myself and turned back to the dollhouse. What an ego I had! I could at least wait to be asked before I decided to turn these hordes of men down.

I needed money for Christmas.

What I really craved was an after-school job, but with eleven hundred college men in a small town, most of whom are desperate for extra income, after school jobs are non-existent.

Which is why I signed up for the psychology department experiment.

The college is always sending sign-up sheets over to the high school science classes. They need volunteers over sixteen for everything under the sun. (Or snow, as the case may be.) They want you to save your urine for six days while you're following a special diet; they need samples of your blood; they want to scan your brain while you sleep; they expect you to answer one hundred questions dealing with your perceptions of right and wrong.

I did one of their diet things once because the only way they could get anybody to follow it was to pay each volunteer ten dollars. Frankly, when it was over I would rather not have had the ten dollars.

But this was different. The psych department was going to test whether lie detectors really worked, and anybody who beat the lie detector would get fifty dollars! There's an incentive we can all respond to. Naturally I went right over to sign up. Apparently the chance to win fifty dollars (not to mention the intrigue of being hooked up to a lie detector) was pretty appealing. The sheet had only twenty slots and nineteen of them were taken. I scribbled my name in the last slot, and it was only after I'd signed in that I saw Jamie Winter's name above mine.

Naturally Hope Martin, who was also willing to lie to get fifty dollars, was standing behind me and noticed. "So that's why you're signing up," she said. "You'd get so much more satisfaction out of dating an older man."

"I am not dating Jamie Winter," I said through clenched teeth. "I am not even seeing Jamie Winter."

"You're trying hard enough," said Hope.

"Hope," I said, deleting all the words my father would not want me to say, "dry up and blow away."

She laughed. "Holly, for your own good, look at what you're doing. You don't want to bother getting out and meeting new people. You're too lazy to socialize with the rest of us. Therefore, you settle for a kid who poses no difficulties for you, and you —"

It was either walk away or kick her in the shins, and because I did not wish to be grounded any longer than necessary I chose walking away. I will not lose my temper, I told myself. I don't care about Hope Martin's opinions. I signed up to try for fifty dollars for Christmas money. I am not trying to get to know Jamie Winter better. Nor am I a lazy clod who won't socialize with acceptable people and settles for kids!

I stomped home, crushing Hope with every crackle of ice.

"You?" said Christopher, laughing heartily. "Beat a lie detector?"

"I might."

"Not a chance. You're like Abraham Lincoln. You'd walk five miles to return the odd penny."

"I told Dad I was going to play Monopoly when I was really going to a movie."

"That's true," said Christopher, "but it was a fluke. You were riddled with guilt doing that. Mom and Dad would have seen it if they hadn't been watching the news when you told them about the Monopoly game. Look at the way you enjoy being grounded."

Enjoy being grounded. Showed what he knew.

All week I thought about the best way to tell lies. I didn't know how a lie detector worked, so it was hard to come up with a plan to beat it. Instead, I planned the spending of the fifty dollars.

Of course, on Sunday my father's sermon was about Christmas giving. We were collecting for migrant workers in the Southwest. "Sometimes," said my father in a slow, sad voice, "these families live in windowless shacks for weeks at a time." He surveyed an unwilling congregation until they all began to fidget. "What would it be like to have no windows? No electrical appliances?" People began reading the backs of their service leaflets, to get away from the sermon. He was going to ask for money again, and nobody wanted to hear about it. "If all of us gave a dollar for every window, bed, clean sheet, and new toy in our houses, how we could help the poor!" said my father.

Two hundred people shifted guiltily in their pews.

I thought of the oriental rug I'd been yearning to put in my dollhouse parlor, and I thought of skinny children hanging in the doorways of their shacks and how my fifty dollars could put sturdy shoes on their cold little feet. The trouble is, I thought, I'm so shallow and worthless that I would rather have the oriental rug.

Maybe it would be best not to win the fifty dollars. Then I wouldn't have all these wrenching financial decisions to make.

Seven

In homeroom, when I had finally peeled off all the layers required to protect my fragile flesh from a temperature hovering at ten degrees and a wind that howled through every scrap of fabric, Hope said timidly, "Holly?"

I thought she had laryngitis. "What?" I felt very strong. I was even prepared to be nice to Hope that day. I had decided that if I won the fifty dollars I would give half to the migrant workers. Nobody could expect more of me than that, and I could still afford the miniature oriental rug and the tiny electrified wall sconces.

"Do you remember a few weeks ago when

Grey came to pick me up after school in a silver Corvette?"

Vividly. The silver Corvette had been absolutely beautiful. Just to be mean I wanted to say, no, I can't remember, how boring. "Yes," I said. I thought, Come *on*, Holly, practice *lying*.

"It wasn't Grey's car, you know. He has a Chevrolet."

It was not like Hope to make Grey sound ordinary. Perhaps Hope was breaking up with Grey in order to date the silver Corvette.

"The guy with the Corvette is a fraternity brother of Grey's," said Hope. "A really gorgeous man. His name is Jonathan Byerly."

"Oh." So now Hope had *two* handsome, rich college men on her string. Really, it was depressing. How come nobody ever wanted old Holly Carroll? I had lots of fine qualities, I was sure of it. Untapped gold mine, that's me, I told myself, and congratulated myself on finally telling a good lie.

"Jonathan noticed you at the bus stop," said Hope, her voice getting timid again. "He thought you had beautiful hair. You were wearing it in one very long French braid that day, down the middle of your back, and Jonathan said it reflected red highlights in the sun. He wondered who you were, and I told him a little bit about you."

I thanked God that Hope knew nothing of my dollhouse. I hadn't worn the single long braid since Christopher said it made me look like Heidi and all I needed were a mountain, some goats, and a cheese.

"Jonathan," said Hope, "would like to date you. He wanted to know if I would fix it up."

If she had thrown herself down the non-existent stairs of her ranch house, she couldn't have surprised me more. I looked at her searchingly. She had a new expression on her face. Not superior but hesitant.

"Jonathan said you sounded like the first interesting girl he'd heard of in this town," said Hope.

I could not imagine what Hope had said to make Jonathan think that. Clearly, Hope could not imagine what she had said either.

"Jonathan's on a full scholarship in the pre-med program," said Hope. "He hates northern New Hampshire but he has to be here."

Jonathan was a brilliant premed student who hated cold climates and drove a silver Corvette? Had I asked only the day before for perfection?

"I told him I'd fix it up," said Hope, and then I understood her timidity. She was afraid I'd refuse and then this Jonathan and her Grey would be annoyed with her. Refuse? I thought. Am I crazy?

I considered Jonathan. "If he's on scholarship, how come he can afford a Corvette?"

"He can't. That's his aunt's. His aunt is Dr. Chambliss, you know. In the physics department. The lady who won that prize last year for whatever it was."

I remembered. My mother spoke of Dr. Chambliss with awe and respect. Dr. Chambliss was the kind of woman my mother would like me to become. It seemed unlikely. "Jonathan wants to date me," I said. It was so impossible I couldn't even get excited about it.

"He does," said Hope, finding it difficult to believe. "He wants to meet you in the Pewter Pot after school."

The Pewter Pot serves fifty kinds of muffins, bagels, and doughnuts with coffee, hot chocolate, or milkshakes. It's a very crowded, very hot little hole in the wall that is a college tradition. All the alums hang out there when they come for reunions. You don't go to the Pew without a date, and usually you don't go there at all unless you're in college or an alum. The Pew is silently acknowledged to be off limits to high school kids.

The Pew.

With Jonathan the brilliant premed student and his silver Corvette.

But I was grounded. I maintained silence

and tried to think of a way around this problem.

"Jonathan is a super person," said Hope. "I'm not kidding, Holly. He's fantastic."

Hope had very high standards in men. If she said he was fantastic, he was fantastic.

"What year is he in school?" I said, stalling. I absolutely hated discussing my father and our family rules with a person like Hope, who seemed to have neither family nor rules.

"A junior. Like Grey. He's twenty-one."

My father would go up in smoke. His daughter? Dating a twenty-one-year-old college man with a silver Corvette? Even being Dr. Chambliss's nephew would not make up for being twenty-one.

And I had to admit that twenty-one sounded pretty old even to me. I didn't like Grey, cute and suave though he was. Why would I like his pal Jonathan? On the other hand, a man whose heart began to churn at the mere sight of sunlight on my brown braid was not a man to be discarded lightly.

"Holly," wailed Hope, "I promised Jonathan I would arrange it."

I had always wanted to be in the position of depriving Hope of something she wanted. Now I was there, and it didn't turn out to be as much fun as I'd anticipated.

All day long I thought about Jonathan instead of classwork.

He sounded like an illustration for a magazine article on eligible men. Maybe Hope had made him up and this was an intricate plot to humiliate me.

For this Jonathan, I actually flunked a Spanish quiz. Me, Holly Carroll, who gets straight 100's in Spanish. The teacher wanted to know if I was ill. She even offered, rather anxiously, to give me a make-up. I just smiled at her weakly and tried to look ill and deserving of a make-up without actually lying about it.

My week was too full of lies.

"Okay," I said to Hope. "I can miss the bus and not be too late. I'll meet Jonathan on the steps after school. That way he can drive me home and we can talk, and he can see if he wants to approach my father."

"Approach your father!" snorted Hope. "You make it sound like *Jane Eyre* or something. Bringing your father in is crazy. You know he'll say no, so why even get him involved in this?"

Every girl except me seemed to be able to run her own life without bothering about parental approval. It really was beginning to get to me. College, I thought grimly. In less than a year I'll be away at college and I can make my own decisions.

I wondered what Jonathan would be like. He'd have to like my shining hair an awful lot to face a minister and beg to be allowed to date his daughter. I pictured that.

A suitor on bended knee. Neat.

Eight

Jonathan.

Well, there turned out to be only one adjective to apply to Jonathan, and it was not one of Hope's.

Yes, he was handsome. Yes, he was definitely driving a silver Corvette. Yes, I knew by the books piled in the backseat that he was a premed student.

But he was also old.

He looked as if I could babysit for his children. Maybe he was only twenty-one, but if so, he was a very mature twenty-one. He made me feel like a Brownie Scout with my camp director. I could accept a ride home with the man, but a *date*? I didn't know whether to laugh or to cry.

Lord, let me think of the right things to say, I prayed. Let me get out of this without calling him Mr. Byerly.

"What's the matter with you?" hissed Hope in my ear. "Holly, he's a dream to look at."

This was true. A full-color poster of Jonathan and his Corvette would be nice to have on my bedroom wall, just to daydream over. But in real life, dark and smooth and fashionable . . . Jonathan looked like someone my *mother* would want a poster of.

"Hello, Holly," said Jonathan Byerly in a middle-aged voice. "What a pleasure to meet you at last."

It was going to be impossible to call him Jonathan. What he was, was Mr. Byerly. "Hi," I said. I blushed. I had never in my whole life felt so *young*. I even had ribbons in my hair. I still had braces on my lower jaw where you couldn't see them, but they marked me "Kid — still getting repairs for adulthood."

"We can get acquainted while I drive you home," said Jonathan. He made getting acquainted sound like an act requiring a cup of tea and a butler. "Hope was telling me about your father. He sounds quite medieval."

I could hardly tell Jonathan that I thought

he sounded pretty medieval himself. I smiled in a sickly fashion, and Hope sort of shoveled me into my side of the Corvette and glared at me very quickly when Jonathan was getting in the other side, just so I'd know I'd better shape up, and fast.

Shape up? I thought hysterically. Into what? An old lady?

We pulled away from the curb, and I tried to think of one thing to say to a man who seemed the right age to be the principal of the school. Nothing whatsoever came to mind.

Jonathan gave me a lovely smile — he, too, had worn braces at some time in the distant, foggy past; it was a perfect smile — and launched into a long description of the nasty weather we'd been experiencing . . . in Spanish.

Now, after four years and straight A's, I am pretty fluent. But he sounded so *affected*. I could not bring myself to respond in Spanish. Lamely, feeling utterly stupid, I said — in English — "Yes, it is pretty cold."

He looked at me in surprise. "Thought you were a Spanish wizard," he said.

"Oh. Well, I guess I do get good grades. I, ah, I guess I don't chat much in Spanish, though."

We had driven one block, and I felt as if

I had been in the front seat of that car forever. My cheeks were burning and my stomach was clenched.

"Where do you live?" he said.

I gave him the worst directions imaginable. I said, "Well, you know, off by the church. You know, where, um, the red light is? Except it's green now. Well, yellow. Turn there. Turn left, I mean. Yes, there, right."

Bad enough to be seventeen with this guy. I *sounded* about three.

Jonathan cleared his throat. "I hear you're not much of a sports fan."

"No," I said and scoured my brain for something to add, but since I wasn't a sports fan I had nothing to say about it.

Jonathan tried again. "Given much thought to where you'll go to college next year?"

"Uh, well, yes, I guess I have. As long as it's hot, you know. I mean, I don't care about the college. As long as I'm warm, you know." I struggled to make myself sound sensible. "I get cold easily," I said.

"You're picking a college based on whether you can get warm there?" said Jonathan.

It sounded insane, when he summarized it for me. "Well," I said. I found myself playing with my braid. I haven't done *that* since elementary school when I used to suck on the tips.

By now we were at my house. Jonathan rolled very slowly up to the curb and let the motor idle for a moment, as though he were trying to decide whether he should park or not. Finally he turned the motor off. Don't let him come in, I thought. Don't let him talk to my father. I'd rather be struck by lightning.

Jonathan handed out yet another topic of conversation. I took a deep breath and tried to sound interesting and logical and sounded stupid and empty instead. I prayed to God to let me think of something to say, but evidently He was off feeding the poor.

"Well," I said, finally. "Um. Thanks for driving me home."

Jonathan was looking at me incredulously, and slowly his expression changed to amusement. I knew exactly what he was laughing at. Himself. For wasting time on some silly little girl just because her hair shone in the sun.

I will never never never never wear my hair like this again, I thought. "Bye," I said frantically, and I fled up to the porch. I didn't even have to fumble for my key because Christopher had gotten home already and was opening the door to see who in the world had driven me home in a silver Corvette. Christopher gaped. "Holly, what —"

"I never want to talk about it. Ever."

I shoved past Christopher, who stood in the

doorway staring out at Jonathan as if the man were a zoo exhibit, and Jonathan, shaking his head and smiling to himself, drove slowly away.

I sagged against the hallway wallpaper and thought about what Jonathan would say to Grey, who would report it to Hope, who would tell the entire word. It was enough to make a girl sick.

I fixed myself a terrific snack to make myself feel better. I think food is the answer to half the world's problems. Leftover cheesecake with a scoop of canned cherry pie filling on top and a glass of ginger ale can unclench even the ulcerating stomach.

I let the first mouthful sit in my mouth and slide slowly down my throat, and I told myself I would live through this; this, too, would pass; eventually the memory of Jonathan would be nothing but a dim blur.

The phone rang. If it was Kate wanting to know who that was in the silver Corvette, I would just change the subject. I had another bite of cheesecake.

"Holly," said Christopher, in a teasing, singsong voice. "It's your very dear friend Jamie."

I swallowed my cheesecake. "What is?"

"On the telephone," sang Christopher. He dropped his singsong and began smirking. "Got a crush on you, doesn't he, Holly? I think

I'll take the bus tomorrow instead of riding with Josh. I got things to say to Jamie Winter."

Perhaps I should forget about waiting for college to get away from all this. I should quit school now, take a bus to Miami, and find a bilingual secretarial job.

I walked silently past my leering brother and took up the phone. "Hello?" I said, trying to keep my voice utterly blank of meaning.

"Hi, Holly. Jamie. You forget the lie detector test?"

"The lie detector test," I repeated.

"Holly, you're on the list for testing at four-fifteen, and it's four-oh-one now. I'm going in in a moment, and I thought I'd call you because there are at least ten people here hoping you'll be late and they can have your slot for getting the fifty dollars."

Some crush, I thought. I glared at my worthless brother. "Thanks," I said to Jamie. "I'm on my way."

I tugged on my coat and scarf, refused to make explanations to Christopher, shoved another bit of cheesecake in my mouth, pulled my cap on and tucked my offensive braid up into the cap, and ate the last bit of cherry pie filling. Then I gulped the last of the ginger ale, wiped my mouth on a napkin, pulled on boots and mittens, flung open the back door, and tore off through the yard. "That's what

I like to see!" yelled Christopher after me. "A girl in the grips of true passionate love. Running all the way to see Jamie!"

"Christopher!" I screamed back at him. "You shut up!" Our backyard is adjacent to the campus, and the Psych building is only a few blocks west. I lurched and leaped through the treacherous paths students had tramped into the old, crusty snow. I put Jonathan, dates, younger men, older men, and hot weather campuses out of my mind and concentrated on my fibbing skills.

N^{ine}

When I got there, panting and gasping for breath, Jamie had already gone in for testing. I flung myself into a chair and began the winter clothes stripping process. Actually, I don't wear nearly as many clothes as I'd like, because people tease me if I wear, for example, three scarves. I do wear two pairs of socks, though. Nobody can see those. I just look as if I have fat feet.

"Holly Carroll?" said the tester in a dry, middle-aged voice.

For one awful minute I thought it was Jonathan, but it was merely the voice that was cloned. The tester was plain and ordinary. "Yes, sir," I said.

"This way, please."

The lie detector test was fun. After they attached little electrodes to various places on my body, they showed me three small objects: a key, a nickel, and a paper clip. "You're going to steal one of these," said the college boy who seemed to be running things. He looked much younger than Jonathan. Perhaps Jonathan had lied about his age and was really thirty-six. Making Jonathan thirty-six made me feel much better. "When we leave you alone in here," the boy went on, "take one of the objects and put it in your shoe. Place the other two back in the box and close the lid. That way we, your testers, cannot tell which object you stole. Then we're going to come back to ask a long series of questions. The first set will be things like, What is the capital of the United States? and, Are you eleven feet tall? You'll lie to some and tell the truth to others, and we'll see what your pattern looks like."

He showed me a needle gently coasting over some graph paper.

"Next, we begin the real questioning," he said. He seemed totally bored. I wondered if I was a boring subject, or if the experiment bored him, or if it was just the proper tone of voice to take when dealing with potential thieves. "We'll be asking all sorts of questions, in an attempt to discover which of these three objects — the key, the nickel, or the paper clip — you actually stole. Keep in mind the fifty dollars, now, and remember that it is to your advantage to lie successfully, just as if you were a criminal risking prison. Right?"

"Right," I said, feeling rather excited.

When I was alone in the room, I settled on the paper clip to steal. My mother is always accusing me of stealing paper clips from her desk anyhow, so I thought perhaps my subconscious would not regard this as a theft and my heart would be totally relaxed when they asked me about stealing the paper clip.

Oh, you're such a crafty little kid, I said to myself. Even if you can't speak in complete sentences around twenty-one-year-old men in Corvettes.

"Did you steal the nickel?" said the tester.

"Yes," I lied cheerfully, picturing my fifty dollars.

"Do you have the key in your shoe?" he said.

"No," I said truthfully.

"Sit still," he said irritably, totally unaffected by my lovely, shiny brown hair. Except for my parents and Jonathan, nobody ever *had* been impressed by that hair. Perhaps they all had vision problems. I decided not to worry about old Jonathan. As for Hope's teasing, that would be nothing new. I'd lived with that since the beginning of time. Or at least, it *felt* like the beginning of time.

"Did you steal the nickel?" said the tester again.

"Yes," I lied again. I decided against buying miniatures. I wanted a new pair of gold earrings. Heart shapes on hoops, like Lydia had.

"Okay," said the tester, "thanks, Miss Carroll. All done."

"How'd I do?" I said eagerly.

He smiled at me. "Don't have a criminal career," he said. "You're as transparent as glass. May I have the paper clip back for the next volunteer, please?"

I walked slowly out of the test room, seeing myself in a new light. Transparent as glass. How unattractive. Jamie was sitting there, alone in a room. All would-be untested thieves had given up and gone home. "Hi," I said gloomily.

"How'd you do?" he asked me, which I thought was quite unnecessary. If I'd won the fifty dollars I'd have been doing pirouettes.

"Lost."

He grinned at me — not a superior grin, but a bubbly, eager grin that made him look like both Kate and Christopher — an unlikely combination if I ever heard of one. I couldn't help grinning back. "You beat it, didn't you?" I said.

He beamed at me. "Sure did. I stole the nickel, and they were convinced I took the key."

"Fantastic! You're rich! How did you do it? Did you have a technique, or are you a natural born liar?" I said.

"I had a technique. Although I put the nickel in my shoes, I kept saying to myself, *Stealing keys! Disgusting. Low. Immoral. That's a crime, James Winter, stealing keys, and you should be ashamed of yourself.* I convinced my heart, I guess, because the lie detector proclaimed that I actually had stolen the key!"

I shook hands with him. "I'm glad to know somebody devious and mysterious," I said. "I myself rated transparent as glass."

We walked out of the Psych building together, laughing and talking. "What are you going to do with the fifty dollars?" I said enviously.

"I really don't know for sure. Want to break it by having a muffin with me at the Pew?"

"I thought the Pew was college territory," I said.

Jamie laughed. "The Pew is in the muffin business. They wouldn't care if vampires sat there as long as they bought muffins. I go to the Pew all the time. Other people like French fries best, or pizza, or ice cream bars, or candy. I like muffins with butter."

"That's not a very fitting food for a successful thief," I said. "Corn muffins are too tame."

"I usually eat blueberry. Although apple, and cheese, and bran muffins are good, too. As long as I can butter them. I belong to the slathering school of thought," Jamie explained. "If it comes out of an oven it needs butter."

"A cholesterol fiend," I said. "Do you know I've been to the Pew only twice in my life, and I've lived here all my seventeen years?"

He shook his head in amazement. "That's why you're so slim, then," he said. "You've never discovered the joys of butter melting on the Pew muffins."

Me. Slim. In fact — *so* slim, was what he'd said. I liked it so much I no longer wanted butter on my muffin, so I could *stay* slim.

We walked the long way, so we'd be on cleared sidewalks and not have to churn through the crusty snow and ice. Jamie began telling me some of his thoughts on spending the fifty dollars. His hobby, it turned out, was steam engines. He had small steam engines mounted on boards to run miniature trains and light bulbs and whistles, and right now he had his eye on an antique threshing machine that had a steam engine.

"A threshing machine?" I said, sure I had misunderstood. "A real one? As big as a house?"

"Well, they're not quite that big, but yes, a real one. The owner doesn't want it. In fact, he hasn't wanted it for forty years. For fifty dollars I could get it towed to my backyard and begin a lifetime project of restoring it to its former glory."

It was difficult to imagine a threshing machine having *any* glory, former or present. Bringing an antique threshing machine home? One presumably covered with rust and filth and having a cracked boiler and missing some parts? "What will your parents say?" I wanted to know. I didn't know Jamie's parents at all. They attended church approximately once every two years, and Mr. Winter frowned steadily for the occasion, but whether he frowned at all things or just church, I didn't know.

"They'd probably like it even less than they did when I got a steam tractor. My tractor's a little on the decrepit side. Every time I plow the garden, my mother's terrified the boiler's going to blow up in my face and leave me blind and scarred for life." He said this nonchalantly, as if discussing a hangnail. "What will your father say?" I asked.

Jamie looked away from me and his face

tightened. "Nothing very nice," he said after a bit. His sweet, buoyant voice sounded almost dead. I saw Mr. Winter frowning, frowning about everything, never saying anything nice, and I shivered slightly. "What will you do with the threshing machine after you get it? Thresh?" I said lightly. "I mean, you don't have a farm."

He paused for another second, and I could almost see him placing his father on a shelf. "I'll just fix it up. I like steam engines. It's a nice, simple, sensible form of energy, and it makes such a satisfying rhythmic noise, too." We discussed collecting. I had a thimble collector in the family (my grandmother) and a Coca-Cola collector living next door, but I had not known there were also old tool, old machine, old farm implement, and even old computer collectors. Jamie himself preferred steam engine collecting. "What's your hobby?" he said, implying that all interesting people had fascinating hobbies and therefore he knew that I would, too.

We were already in the Pew, seated and ordering, and I had hardly noticed the college boys littering the place. With Jonathan I had been so embarrassed I could hardly move my lips, but with Jamie I was just enjoying myself tremendously. Of course, Jamie wasn't a date.

And he was also just a junior who didn't matter particularly. That helped.

I had one sick moment when I imagined I saw Jonathan in the back booth of the Pew, but it wasn't Jonathan, just some middle-aged man with the same color jacket, and I breathed easier. I told Jamie about my dollhouse and the furniture I'd made for it and the almost-finished Christmas tree I was painting and the gazebo I was still sketching out on graph paper.

Jamie quizzed me a bit, to be sure I really did know what a lathe was for and when to use a jigsaw, and his eyes stopped blinking and for a moment he stared at me narrowly, as if rethinking his position on me.

I buttered another blueberry muffin and savored my hot chocolate. I could see how a person could develop an affection for the Pew food.

"Oh, no!" I said. "Oh, Jamie, I'm grounded! For going to see that movie I told you about! I'm not supposed to be here. Dad was so upset with me for betraying his trust, as he put it. I've got to fly home."

Jamie just smiled. "I'll go home with you and make excuses. Your father and I are old friends. I really don't think he'd mind that we had a muffin together at the Pew for half an hour."

"You and Dad are old friends?"

"Sure. He's good to talk to."

I stared at Jamie. "About what?"

"Oh, you know. Life. Truth. That kind of thing. How about it? Want me to walk you home?"

It was one thing to meet by coincidence at the Psych building. One thing to celebrate Jamie's win at the Pew. It was something else again to walk home together as the dusk darkened the streets and the chill went into the bone and you naturally walked closer. Christopher didn't even like Jamie, for some reason, and would jump to conclusions and be ready and willing to tease us forever. And there was Hope, who would have it in for me already after the Jonathan fiasco and would love to get her teeth into a "Dating a junior, Holly? Really, how immature you are!" scene.

"That's okay, Jamie," I said nervously. "It's getting late and your house is in the opposite direction. Thanks for the muffins. I had such a nice time. And congratulations on winning! I'm truly impressed." I kept talking on and on, as if we were parting forever and I had to wrap up the loose ends of my entire life.

Finally I managed to stop babbling. Jamie was just grinning at me. "You're welcome," he said. "See you." He turned and walked off toward his house.

I felt incredibly lonely, seeing him go. He was broad-shouldered, as big as Stein and Beaulieu and the others on the hockey team. He doesn't look sixteen, I thought. I took one step after him. "Jamie?" I called.

He looked back at me, with his same sweet grin. "What?"

And then I didn't know why I had called after him. I flushed and stammered a moment. "You aren't really going to put an antique threshing machine in the backyard, are you?"

"Probably not. My father's reached his limit with that hobby. But it's nice to daydream, don't you think?"

I definitely thought. He daydreams, too, I thought. I felt vaguely giddy. We said good-bye again, and more quickly this time, as the sun was gone and the air was turning downright hostile with night cold, and I went home alone.

Ten

I love Christmas.

The gaudy lights, shaped like enormous bells, that are hung each year from the telephone poles in the village. The streams of jazzed-up carols piped through every store. The window decorations with their pretend snow and their flickering lights. Candles on the table and shiny wrapping paper and curling ribbons and bows.

I love it all.

In church we hung beautiful evergreen wreaths around the old copper wall sconces and tied them with fragrant winter apples and tiny, scarlet velvet bows. For me, it was the smell of Christmas: apples and pine.

My father, who frets over everything, worries each year that someone in the village, or from the college, will be alone Christmas Day, and that sounds so awful to him that he extends invitations to anyone who might possibly require the company of strangers for Christmas dinner. So this year our table seated a few stray foreign students (including a confused Hindu and a fascinated Moslem), a few students too broke to fly home for the holidays, a couple of elderly widows, one man in his fifties whose wife had just left him after thirty years of marriage, and my grandmother.

It was a wonderful meal, with wonderful conversation, and I noticed that Christopher and I had passed out of our embarrassed stage. For years we blushed when Dad prayed, and ducked our heads when he read from Luke, and tried to leave when he lit the Advent candles. But this year I just loved it. As the strangers at our table added their prayers for peace, I thought of Jamie, and what sort of things he might have talked about with my father, and I saw my own father differently: as the sort of man Jamie would consider a friend.

Dad was especially happy because the church had given almost half again as much money for the migrants as he'd asked for, and so he felt he really *was* accomplishing something in this wicked world. My mother made no comments, just smiled. I don't think she's one fraction as religious as Dad, but she won't hurt his feelings or confuse the issue by saying it. I hoped that in a few years my mother and I would discuss things like that. Or even this year. Seventeen was adult.

I had loads of lovely gifts. Long, dangling gold filigree earrings from my grandmother — the sort you'd wear with a satin gown at the party of the year. Two beautiful sweaters — soft pastel knits with creamy snowflake patterns. New boots — thick, furry, lined boots to keep even *my* toes warm. Beautiful, tiny velvet draperies for the drawing room of my Victorian mansion. Dad had made me an octagonal Shaker barn to go with the mansion. It was a triumph of woodworking, although not precisely a period match.

"A whole new world!" I said. "Now I'll need tiny fences and shrubbery and miniature paving bricks for paths. I can make hay from yellow broom tips."

Christopher handed me a package. He'd bought me a flock of miniature china chickens and one gaudy old china rooster looking ready to peck my fingers! "I thought we'd put the dollhouse on a four by eight piece of plywood," said Dad, "and you can make a yard and have the barn out back and leave a space for that gazebo you're planning."

Even if it came in winter, Christmas was wonderful!

I went upstairs to put on the new earrings. All my others were costume jewelry — enameled scarlet hearts, miniature crayons, preppy alligators, and that sort of thing. I slid into a wonderful daydream about the sort of dances and dates I'd have in the New Year where my grandmother's filigree gold earrings would be just right. I could see myself swirling on a dance floor, sparkling like a princess.

Downstairs I listened to the prayers for peace. Our Indian and Iraqi guests prayed in their own languages, and Mother spoke some old Latin prayers, and one of the students, a French major, prayed in French.

Christopher had vanished outdoors. I'd gotten him a pair of snowshoes, and he was wild with excitement. My mother worried a little, looking out into lightly falling snow and talking of trackless wilderness in which Christopher could get lost, but actually we could see him just fine tramping across the college campus.

A white Christmas. Two years (to the grief of the ski industry) since our last white Christmas. I sat indoors and dreamed and thought of peace and love.

On December twenty-sixth, I called Kate to see what she'd gotten and whether we could get together. She'd gotten the new ski boots she was yearning for and had left very, very early to get a space on the slopes. I called Lydia, but she'd gone with her boyfriend to work on their ice sculpture.

I called two other girls. They were both out. One was skiing with Kate, and the other had gone to a hill to take her little brother and sister sledding.

I sat in my bedroom and stared at my dollhouse and my lovely sweaters and the soft bubbly feeling of Christmas dwindled away. Christopher was out with his friends. My father was checking on three families he thought might be short of money to order fuel oil, and my mother was correcting term papers. Grandmother was back in Boston.

It was a long day. Longer than any I could remember.

I had plenty of projects I could start. Dollhouse stuff. A kit from my uncle in Milwaukee for making Ukrainian Easter eggs: the kind with intricate designs on them. Some strange, rough-feeling but beautiful knitting wool from a sheep farm near us.

But I was not in a crafts mood. I was in a company mood. I wanted to talk to a friend.

I thought about telephoning Jamie, just to talk.

Would it be as easy on the telephone as it was in person? Would we start laughing and telling stories right away? Or would he be startled and unable to figure out what I was doing on the line? Would he think I was chasing him? Be horrified and embarrassed?

I wondered whether his parents had let him tow an antique threshing machine into the yard. What sort of gifts had been given Christmas Day to a boy who was crazy about steam engines?

For supper, we had leftover ham and warmed-up sweet potatoes. It had such a day-after feeling to it. I couldn't even finish eating.

When the telephone rang I knew it was for somebody else. It felt like years since anybody had shown any interest in me, and I dragged myself around the table, clearing it, thinking that the only thing anybody wanted Holly Carroll for was doing the dishes.

"For you, Holl," said my brother.

Jamie? I thought, and the thought surprised me. Why should *he* call? Why should I even think that he might? "Who is it?" I said.

"Kate." Christopher doesn't care for Kate. She's going to be eighteen next month and once or twice, when Christopher was ten or eleven, she actually babysat for him. Why, Kate's almost two years older than Jamie, too, I thought. No wonder she thinks of him as a kid.

"Hi, Kate. Have a good Christmas?"

"Super." She told me every detail, concentrating on how wonderful the skiing had been that day, and how they had oversold tickets, so that there were infuriating lines at the lifts, but still, she had had a ball and everybody had been there, everybody but me. "Hollyberry," she said, "come skating with us tomorrow? The temperature is going to be up in the high twenties with no wind, and the sun shining so it'll be really very comfortable. Come on, please?"

It's pretty bad when your best friend has to hear a weather report before she dares invite you anywhere. "I'd love to," I said, and I made a mental note never to mention weather again. Hope and Christopher were right: I was a bore, the way I kept whining about the frigid air outdoors.

"Do your old skates fit?" said Kate anxiously. "Mom says you can wear hers."

Kate and her mother had talked over how to get me to the skating party. It warmed me right down to my toes, being wanted like that.

"Great," I said. "Mine are a little crunchy around the toes."

We giggled. I forgot about Jamie. What I'd needed all day was a friend, and Kate was the best friend I had.

Eleven

Kate's mother's skates were just a fraction too big, and even with two pairs of socks and the ankles laced as tight as my fingers could pull, I didn't have enough ankle support. I hadn't skated once that year, and I was very rusty.

I wound slowly around the pond, getting my coordination back, and I was circling for the fourth time when Christopher came gliding toward me at full speed, making faces and yelling, "Is that slow-moving vehicle actually my sister?" I tried to veer away from him, but of course he didn't really plan to bump me, and he veered in the same direction. We crashed right into each other, and even before

I heard my ankle hit the ice I knew the bone was going to break.

Christopher just bounced a little and was back on his skates in the space of an instant, but I took a terrible spill, turning my ankle under me with a crack that sounded as if the ice was splitting. Half the skaters heard it and turned, cringing, to see who it was.

It hurt so much I literally could not speak. I could not untwist myself from my fallen position, and the skate kept my ankle in a horrid unnatural curve.

"Somebody call an ambulance," said a voice. "She's really hurt."

Christopher hunched down beside me, white and horrified. "Oh, Holly," he said desperately, "I'm sorry, I was only teasing."

I couldn't even moan. The breath had been knocked so completely out of me it was all I could do to breathe. Tears sprang into my eyes, from cold and pain and shame, and when the ambulance attendants unwrapped my legs and straightened me out, I bit right through my mittens trying to hold back the scream.

In the ambulance they unlaced the skate, and I really thought I would die. It felt as if they were amputating my ankle with a wood-saw.

"Oh, does it hurt that much?" said the ambulance attendant.

I tried to laugh but I sobbed instead. When I saw the needle coming toward me I almost leaned into the shot, I wanted the pain relief so much.

I will say two things for the hospital.

First, it was warm. No drafts or subzero temperatures on the orthopedic floors!

Second, it was full of friends. Everybody came to visit me. You practically had to have reservations, like for the ski lift. I had so much fun it was almost worth the broken ankle! Writing on my plaster cast was the most popular activity during the last week of the Christmas holidays. Even Hope and Grey came, and Grey turned out to be a budding cartoonist — he drew cute little cats hobbling around on crutches, and sprinkled the cats among all the signatures. "Jonathan says hi," Grey told me.

"Oh," I said, flushing. "Tell him hi back."

Fortunately my mother came in, saying hello to Hope, and Grey had to be introduced, so I was spared any details about Jonathan.

Jamie came the third day. I'd been thinking about him, and then stopping myself from thinking about him. And there he was.

"Got your ticket out of winter sports, I see," he said.

"Get one yourself," I suggested. "Plenty of empty beds."

"No, thanks! Maybe during final exams, but never, never during a school vacation!"

We gave each other enormous grins. I noticed all sorts of details about him I'd never seen before: how his hair parted unevenly and fell in floppy, soft blond waves. How he had a habit of tugging at his lips, as if he had another grin coming and he didn't want it to emerge just yet. How he was obviously still growing, because even what were evidently his new Christmas clothes seemed too short at the wrists and too narrow at the shoulders. "You get your threshing machine?" I said.

"Nope. My mother said we weren't even going to discuss anything as ridiculous as that, and my father said — well, it's probably best to delete anything my father says. So how was your Christmas, Holly?"

We talked about Christmas. School. Life. Careers. Hobbies. We even got into heavy things — like people suffering while we were fat and happy. About volunteering and charities and religions. Then we fell back onto school topics again.

"I'm sure school has a purpose," said Jamie morosely, "but this year it's much harder to discern."

"I know what you mean. Every single subject that comes up, I think to myself — do I care? And the answer is — no."

"Always excepting Spanish, right?"

"That's right. Spanish is an exception. How did you know?"

"Are you kidding? You're a legend in your own time, Holly. The girl who plans her future so thoroughly she knows what climate, what language, and even what nation she'll be emigrating to."

We giggled like little kids. "Yep," I said. "I've got my whole future planned weather-wise. It's the other stuff — like college, career, income, money, that kind of thing — that I haven't solved yet."

We had the best time talking. Jamie brought a funny article from a magazine for me to read, and when I said I'd read it later, he said, no, he wanted me to hear it now. So he read it aloud to me.

He wore reading glasses. I'd never been in a class with Jamie, and I'd never even known about the reading glasses. They aged him. He looked distinguished. Older. Looks like Grey, I thought suddenly. Why, even Hope would approve of Jamie in glasses.

My parents arrived about five and Jamie and I were still talking away. "Well, hi," he said to my parents, obviously pleased to see them.

"How are you?" said my father. He meant it.

"I'm surviving," said Jamie, and they smiled at each other and I was eaten up with curiosity. What had Jamie survived, and how had my father helped him? Jamie seemed so relaxed and sane to me, as if he could not possibly live in a world with problems.

My mother asked how his Aunt Eunice was doing with her cancer chemotherapy treatments. The hospital aides brought in my tray (they eat impossibly early in a hospital; it's enough to make anyone swear off injury and illness), and Jamie said, looking at my meal, "That stuff is greasy enough to lubricate a truck."

We began a series of wisecracks about cafeteria food. He's so good-looking, I thought, staring into his wide, sweet grin. But I can't fall for him. Not for a *junior*.

"Well, I have to go." Jamie got up reluctantly. I loved it — his slowness to get up, the way he still had things to say and jokes to crack. "I guess I'll stop worrying about you, Holl," said Jamie. "For a desperately injured girl, you look pretty terrific."

There was a pause, and I thought if my parents had not been there, Jamie would have bent over the bed and kissed me. I thought if my parents had not been there I might have caught Jamie's hand and *made* him bend over and kiss me — but they were there, and we just looked at each other silently and swallowed and said good-bye uncertainly.

"Mother," I said when he was gone, "this food is not fit for human consumption. I'm going to die of malnutrition. Can you bring me a Big Mac and some French fries?"

I think my mother might have commented on Jamie, or asked if there were any boys I liked these days, or something equally subtle, but my father of course sprang into his lecture about pitiful human beings who really don't have anything to eat, and how I should be grateful even for food greasy enough to lubricate a truck.

Jamie spun around in my head, and his laugh and his jokes ricocheted off the hospital room walls.

I lay in bed that night telling myself that age mattered not at all. That Jamie and I would be the perfect couple and be totally happy together.

But I kept seeing the cafeteria, with its table for seniors and its table for juniors, and how nobody ever crossed, except a few girls who were next-door neighbors and best friends, and even they didn't do it much.

Twelve

"Winter Mist," said Kate.

I looked at her in confusion, and out at the crowded cafeteria, trying to see something that resembled Winter Mist.

"Lipstick name," she explained. "How do you like it?"

I had sworn off cold weather comments. "Mmmm," I said.

"Ugh," said Lydia. "What color would it actually turn out to be, once you got it on your lips? Slush gray? Sleet white?"

"True," said Kate. "It doesn't exactly grip you with the desire to have your lips that shade. I'm still trying to plan a line of lipsticks for winter. Shades that make you think of lovely lips on ski slopes."

I could not possibly care what color my lips, or anybody else's, were when I had taken my life in my hands to whip down treacherous slopes at insane speeds. Now a ski *lodge* lipstick, that I could imagine.

"Perhaps Winter Apricot," said Kate. "Or Frozen Burgundy."

I could see a shriveled fruit hanging off an ice-killed tree. "Kate," I said, "I think Winter Apricot would be a real seller."

Kate was happy. "Here," she said. "I'll dump your books at this table. You sit on the outside seat so you can sprawl your cast in the aisle and other people can trip over it and have their own personal chance to break bones."

"How neighborly," I said.

Lydia offered to get my lunch tray for me.

"Oh, thanks!" I said. I must say, a lot of friendly service went along with having a foot in a cast. It almost compensated for the deep and painful path the crutches were wearing under my arms. "I'll have the sandwich," I said.

"Holly," said Lydia, in the voice of doom, "it's pimiento cheese."

We contemplated the damp and warm pimiento cheese sandwiches slapped together by our cafeteria staff, a group of overweight sadists who must surely eat somewhere else. Lydia shuddered. "Better have soup and salad. At least the soup comes out of cans."

"They can even ruin that," said Kate glumly. "Add twice as much water so all you get is vegetable-flavored bilge."

In the end I went up to the line myself, so as to be able to choose the least loathsome of the day's selections. Somehow, due to my slowness and their hunger, Kate and Lydia got separated from me in the cafeteria line. When I got a gentle poke in the ribs, I thought it must be Kate telling me to pay attention, the line was moving, pick up those crutches and hobble on . . . but it was Jamie.

I turned and looked at him, and a warm spot of pleasure started in my chest and spread through me. He gave me a one-quarter grin that said a very private *I'm glad to see you.* I gave him the same grin back, and his fingers moved over my ribs again. Half tickle, half caress.

"Carry your tray for you?" he said. Anybody listening would have thought Jamie bored. Merely courteous to some strange girl in difficulties.

"That would be lovely."

He was warm and solid and male, standing behind me in his jeans, the sagging sleeve of his old pullover sweater brushing down my arm, his fingers lightly at my waist. I wanted to say *forget the tray — carry me!*

Lydia, separated from me by two other kids, told them to pass her because she had to be next to me. "It's okay, Lyd," I said. "Someone else volunteered."

She looked once, to see who that might be, and when her eyes found Jamie she lifted one eyebrow at us both. Is that all she's going to say! I thought. I can handle that. Lydia turned her attention to finding the best piece of lemon meringue pie on the dessert rack. I twined my fingers through the handle grip of the wooden crutches and caught Jamie's finger. He drew a snowflake pattern on my palm of my hand and put a soup bowl on my tray with the other hand. "Rolls?" he said.

"Please," I said.

He added ten pats of butter to the single roll on his own tray.

"Uh, Jamie?" I said. "Is that perhaps a little more butter than absolutely necessary?"

"I butter everything," he said, putting a salad on the tray.

"Including lettuce?" I said.

He regarded his salad thoughtfully. "I haven't tried that," he conceded. "But I'm willing to consider it."

My stomach shivered with laughter, but we were conspirators, having a tiny cafeteria-line date, and I didn't want to be trespassed upon. I kept the laughter silent. The line closed in, everybody squeezing to reach a good dessert. I refused one, thinking of buttered lettuce instead, and wishing Jamie and I could spend the afternoon at the Pew where the butter was easy to slather on. When I looked back at him, he was not studying the desserts. Or even getting more butter. He was studying me.

The laughter inside me turned almost to a cramp. Oh, Jamie! I thought. *Gosh, I like you.*

We were at the cash register. I fumbled for my wallet and change and had a hard time balancing. Jamie's huge shoe pushed against the base of the crutches, stabilizing me. I looked down at the shoe and he waved the huge toe of the shoe at me. I had one bare toe protruding from my cast. I waved it back, and I felt Jamie tremble with laughter beside me.

My daydream with my filigree earrings flodded me, and it was Jamie who swirled out with me onto the dance floor. I handed the cafeteria checker my four quarters and wondered what Jamie looked like dressed up. Had I ever even seen him in decent clothes? I tried to remember what he had worn to church two years ago, but two years ago I didn't have a crush on Jamie Winter. The memory was impossible to retrieve. Have to build some memories, I thought. Have to do things with Jamie.

I wanted to look at Jamie so much that I couldn't look at him. I would have cried out or giggled idiotically or blushed a permanent red.

"My, my," said Lydia, in a cool, probing voice. "Starting off the New Year with younger men, eh, Hollyberry?"

The two girls between Lydia and me, a few feet away now with their loaded trays, turned to look at us. They were juniors. I didn't even know their names, but they certainly knew Jamie. They looked at him, interpreted Lydia's remark, and burst out into evil snickers, jabbing each other with sharp elbows before they pranced off for the junior side of the cafeteria.

"Looks heavy," said Lydia, smirking at us.

I wanted to laugh. To say, "You've got it, Lyd old girl. Can't slip anything past you, can we?"

But I didn't.

I said, "Don't be silly, Lydia. He's just carrying the tray."

I could not believe I had said that. I could have bitten off my tongue. *That was no private, special cafeteria-line date, Lydia, that was just a young servant I ordered around. He has no meaning in my life whatsoever.*

Lydia turned, amused, and walked toward our usual table. "Jamie," I whispered, trying to find a sentence to excuse inexcusable words . . . but Jamie was gone. Following Lydia. Carrying my tray. His back was to me.

Gary Beaulieu had come to sit with Kate, who was beaming with delight, and Gary patted the table where he expected Jamie to set my tray. Gary didn't so much as break off his conversation to speak to Jamie, but simply got up to hold a chair out for me, elbowing Jamie away from the table. I looked at Jamie, mutely begging forgiveness, but Jamie wasn't looking at me. He was steering around Gary, his eyes angry and his cheeks taut and red. I wished his shoe would wave at me, forgive me, butter a little lettuce for me, anything at all. But the shoe walked away. I had blown it.

Gary propped my crutches safely out of the way.

I could run after him, I thought wildly. Except I can't run. He could sit here, I thought. Except all eight seats are filled, with seniors.

Jamie was gone. I had not even thanked him for carrying the tray. Tears stung my eyes.

I'd spent an entire week thinking about Jamie and looking forward to seeing him again. First sign of teasing among my friends — or acquaintances, as I would have to term Lydia — and I backed off. What's the matter with me? I thought. Why can't I be honest and be me?

I would never be able to eat lunch. My entire abdomen was knotted like a piece of macrame.

"Holly?" said Gary Beaulieu. "You okay?"

I stared at him through a mist of tears. "Yes. Sure. Thanks."

"You look as if your ankle hurts. The nurse could give you aspirin, you know. Not that aspirin probably does much for broken bones."

"I'm fine," I told him. I began slurping my soup, which was tomato and excellent. Thanks to Campbell's, not the cafeteria.

I burned my tongue on it and was rather glad. I deserved punishment for not standing up for the way I felt about Jamie. Weak, I said to myself. You're weak. Limp. Worthless.

Everybody had cold weather tales to tell. How the thermometer had dipped to twenty-six below at their place. How they'd been forced to spend New Year's Eve trying to get some ski visitor's car started. How their pipes had burst in spite of the new insulation.

And they accuse *me* of thinking too much about winter weather, I thought. I was glad I had missed the bitter cold of the New Year, being laid up in the hospital.

Across the cafeteria I located Jamie. He was sitting with his back to me. I know him from the back, I thought. The thought was very strange. As if I'd been thinking so much about Jamie that even the back of his head was already familiar to me.

He and his junior classmates were eating like hogs and generally behaving like children. Sixteen, I thought. He's only sixteen.

I wondered when his birthday was. When we'd both be seventeen.

Pete Stein tapped my shoulder.

"Hi, Pete," said Gary.

"Hi, Pete," I said. I saw that he had survived yet another few weeks with his front teeth intact. When a person is a hockey goalie, he has to worry about these things. Pete was wearing his ski vest over his oxford shirt, which was the only clothing he ever wore, in school or out. We had chemistry together next period, and I thought he must need to glance at my book for some reason.

"It's two floors up to chemistry," said Stein. "I was thinking what a hard time you'd have getting up the stairs during passing period with a million kids shoving, and I thought maybe we could go on up now and I'll carry your books for you."

"Why, Stein!" I said, surprised. "That's terrific of you."

Stein nodded, agreeing that terrific moments were not unusual for a jock as superior as he.

Gary handed over the crutches, and I was just planning how to haul myself upright without looking totally awkward and clunky when Stein put his hands around my waist and simply lifted me to my feet. I felt like a piece of sports equipment being set in its proper position. Stein straightened me out to his satisfaction. Kate and Lydia made several remarks about how Stein shouldn't stop with that — he should get to know old Hollyberry better in a number of other ways. Fortunately Stein was not listening to them (I don't think he listens much to anybody except his coaches), and after he restacked my books on top of his, we set off for chemistry.

Half the cafeteria was watching us.

Because we were seniors? And seniors are always interesting to freshmen and sophomores and juniors? Because of Kate's and Lydia's wisecracks that had set several tables laughing? Because of my crutches? Or because Stein was a sports hero and everything he did was interesting?

My eyes caught Jamie's, but Jamie looked away so fast the only message I got was lost in transit. Angry, I thought, of course he's angry. My chest hurt, hating myself for being so small and stupid. What does Jamie think of Stein lifting me up? I wondered. Does he know it was simply to speed the progress toward chemistry? Does he think I like Stein better? Does he *care*?

Pete Stein told me all about how he and his uncle and his two cousins had gone camping over Christmas. "Camping?" I said numbly. "But Stein! The temperature at night was close to thirty below zero. And the wind! The wind-chill factor must have brought it to fifty below."

"They estimated sixty," said Stein happily.

I looked at him for traces of insanity or frostbite and found neither.

"We needed to test out our new sleeping bags," he explained. "They were supposed to be fit for arctic weather, so the holidays were perfect for trying them out."

I thought, imagine. Camping. Voluntarily. In this weather. "And were they?" I said. "Perfect, I mean?" I sustained myself up the second flight of stairs with a vision of my future camping expeditions. The Florida Keys, perhaps. White sand for miles, hot blue sky above me, blazing yellow sun turning me a golden tan.

"It was great," said Stein. "Terrific." He helped me negotiate a turn in the stairs. "One more floor," he said, with excessive enthusiasm.

He sounded like a one-man cheering squad. I could just hear him on a hike. *One more mountain, guys. One more blizzard. Isn't this great?*

At last we reached the top. I leaned against the wall for a moment to pant. The cast was very heavy, and dragging it up two flights was very tiring. Stein looked at me edgily. "Never fear," I reassured him. "I am not about to faint on you. Just getting my breath back."

Stein shuddered visibly. At first I thought he was terrified by exhausted women, but then he said, "That broken bone must be awful. You can't do *anything*."

A cast on the foot does not prevent a girl from decorating a dollhouse or watching TV reruns. Stein was thinking of his own life, which was solidly packed with skis, skates, basketballs, hockey pucks, tennis balls, and soccer fields in their seasons.

"I always worry about broken bones," said Stein. "So far I've been real lucky. One broken collarbone and a broken finger, but nothing serious. Never had to have crutches or a sling."

"But every time you participate in one of your sports, you risk it," I objected. "Think of the hockey pucks flying in your face."

"That's what my mother says. She wants me to be a doctor. She says that way it's the *other* people who'll get hurt."

I had not known that Stein was capable of making a joke. I'm always ready to laugh so I laughed. But this turned out to be an error. Stein was not kidding around. He was peeved with his mother for not wholly supporting his athletic future.

Stein was handsome, in a shaggy dog sort of way. I wondered what it would be like to go out with him. It would certainly impress everybody. We wouldn't even have to have fun, or exchange a single interesting remark. All we'd have to do would be appear together and people would be impressed.

What would a girl do with Stein? Other than admire his plays during games, that is. He'd probably ask a girl to go ice fishing, I thought.

Stein glided down the hall, hampered not in the least by my faltering progress. He had that athletic body where every movement seems to involve every perfect muscle, so you always sort of yearn to see him without clothes, so as to admire those muscles working together, like a male chorus.

Now, now, Holly, I said to myself. The only thing you and Stein have in common is that you both breathe. And even *that* you don't do in the same fashion. You're gasping like a fish, and he's probably got a resting pulse of around ten.

Bet he doesn't butter his salad, I thought, and suddenly I wanted fiercely to be back in the cafeteria, replaying the whole scene with Jamie, ignoring Lydia, sitting with the junior boys. The junior boys? No. I wouldn't have done it.

". . . the waterfalls in Swann's Wood," Stein

was saying. "Boy, you should join the Snow-mobile Club, Holly. It was only eight miles cross-country, and that waterfall was so beautiful, frozen solid like that. Nature," said Stein pompously, "at her very best."

I myself prefer people at their very best. Art museums and restaurants, libraries and airplanes, shoe shops and sidewalks.

I pictured Jamie and me sitting in the Pew slathering butter on our blueberry muffins and talking about People versus Nature.

In chemistry our teacher — he's one of those supremely boring teachers you get from time to time — droned on about the test we were to have on Friday. He hoped we had spent our holidays fruitfully pursuing our chemistry texts and memorizing our formulas, he said ominously, because on Friday, we would separate the men from the boys.

What a hateful phrase. I visualized our high school separating its men from its boys, and I could see all too well which line Jamie would end up in. Men were seniors.

Stein grinned at me from his side of the room, as bored by the lecture as I was, and he rolled his eyes at the teacher. I was thinking of Jamie when I flushed, but several kids saw the look Stein gave me and my subsequent blush, and they totally misinterpreted it. Oh, no, I thought. Do I need this?

Lisa, next to me, kept clearing her throat to attract my attention. She leaned down on a crooked elbow to hide her face from the teacher and mouthed at me, *"You and Stein?"*

Her eyes were bright with eagerness. If I nodded — *yes, me and Stein* — she would smother a giggle and grin triumphantly as if she and I had plotted a long campaign to snag Stein and now I had him.

I wondered what Lisa would say if I told her how I felt about Jamie. *Eeeuuuhhh, you like him? But, Holly, he's a junior!*

"Miss Carroll? Did breaking your ankle also deprive you of speech?"

I stared numbly at the teacher and flushed even redder.

"You were asked an important question, Miss Carroll."

"I'm sorry. Could you repeat it, please?" I hate being caught daydreaming. It makes me feel so stupid, and I felt stupid enough for one day.

"No, I could not. Pay attention, Miss Carroll. That's a zero for class participation again today."

Again today? Had I begun making a habit of this kind of thing?

Zero.

Talk about New Year's omens. So far I'd had: Coordination — zero; Boys — zero; School — zero. Sounded like a really successful year coming up.

*T*hirteen

That night when I got home, absolutely drained of all energy and ability, I found the first of my college application blanks waiting for me.

Now, I usually love filling out forms. Sometimes on Sunday I entertain myself by filling out all the book club forms and all the mail order forms in the Sunday paper. I write my name very neatly, centering the middle initial perfectly, and when I get to my street address, I get this tiny little pleasure from how distinctive it is. 17 Featherbed Lane. Now there's an address. Of course, you hear a few raunchy jokes about it and those get pretty tiresome, but it's so antique and Yankee-sounding and it sure beats North Main or Maple Avenue.

I shoveled the trash off half my desk so I'd have a good form-filling-out space and decided that a college application would be good therapy.

I was wrong. There were five pages of blanks. I am not sufficiently interesting for five pages. Five *lines*, maybe.

The only successful spot on the whole page was 17 Featherbed Lane, and that certainly wasn't original with Holly Carroll. The blanks, far from being friendly little white spaces to fill with comforting letter shapes, loomed like a nightmare of gravestones. I was a zero — a nothing — and yet I had to package myself successfully and sell myself to those colleges. On that grayish recycled paper. I had to face the fact that I was not the best student, the most interesting writer of essays, the finest athlete, or the incoming freshman with the most leadership potential. There were going to be all sorts of spaces I'd have to leave blank because *I* was blank.

I pictured Stein filling out his. He'd need extra paper, the way Honor Society types need extra paper during essay tests. I'm there writing three paragraphs in my most sprawling script, and they're writing a book, they know so much.

I must capitalize on my strong points, I told myself firmly. I'm okay, they're okay.

I'm number one. Good in Spanish. Really nice hair. Functions exceptionally well in heat waves.

I left the college form on the desk and wandered over to my dollhouse and its new octagonal barn. I need to cut hay, I told myself. Make some miniature geraniums out of red tissue and green wire, and plant them along the path from the house.

But the pleasure was gone. It was difficult to believe I had ever actually done that sort of thing. Decorated dollhouses and daydreamed of miniature oriental rugs. That sort of occupation was as remote as the five-year-old for whom it had been made. Right now there was room for nothing in my mind but college and Jamie. Also, Jamie and college. And the general worthlessness of Holly Carroll for either.

I got myself so involved in trying to figure out Truth and Who Am I that I got even more depressed and ended up lying on my bed drowning sobs in the pillow.

If Christopher comes into my room right now, I thought, I'll murder him. Then I'll be sent to prison and that will decide the future for me. My career will be making license plates.

I left my room eventually only because I was starving. The only truth I had come upon during my weeping was that food solves a lot of problems. I decided upon an open-faced cheese sandwich. Cheese melting and getting soft and golden brown, running down the sides of a thick slice of whole wheat bread. Yes, the more I considered the toasted cheese sandwich, the more food mattered and the less college did.

Still, when the phone rang, I decided not to answer it. If it wasn't for me, there was no point in rushing to get the call. I chewed another delectable bite of hot cheese and bread. And if it was for me, I wasn't interested in discussing anything with anybody anyhow.

"Holly!" yelled Christopher, with a particularly jeering tone in his voice. Rotten little creepy kid brother, I thought. Why didn't I strangle him back when he was small enough that I could have done it easily? "What?" I bellowed back.

"It's Katie Bait." (An old nickname, from when Kate used to go fishing all the time and Christopher hated her because she babysat for him twice and he wished somebody would go fishing with *her*.)

I got up, cramming the last of the sandwich in my mouth, and went to the phone. Christopher had intelligently withdrawn from the combat area. "Mmhellmo?" I said through the cheese.

"Hollyberry," said Kate excitedly. "Guess what we're doing tomorrow?"

"What?"

"Stein had this great idea. Last week he went over through Swann's Wood to the waterfalls and they're frozen and extremely beautiful and —"

"Nature at her very best," I said.

"What?"

"Nothing. Go on."

"And everybody decided to have a winter picnic by the falls. You and Lydia and Susan and Gary and Stein and me and Ross . . ."

Oh, no, I thought. Oh, no, oh, no.

Kate was as wound up as a violin string. "It'll be so much fun!" she squealed. "And just think, Holly. You can get to know Stein better this way. I'll make sure you share his snowmobile. I think he wants it that way, anyhow. He likes you."

"I know Stein as well as I need to," I said. "I've been in homeroom with him since September seventh, and if there's one thing we feature down in that prison it's intimacy."

"Holly," said Kate, getting annoyed. She sounded like *my* babysitter. I began to identify with Christopher's feelings toward her. "Holly, *Stein likes you*." Intensely, as if we were discussing something important. "Anybody can see that," Kate went on. "If you'd just put some effort into it, you could get Stein to ask you out. And — there's nobody better in the whole senior class!"

There's somebody better in the junior class, I thought. "So drop Gary," I said, being mean, "and go after Stein."

Kate said nothing. I was ashamed of myself again. "I'm sorry, Katie," I said. "It's just that I don't have anything much to say to Pete Stein. I like him okay. He's a fine person. But —"

"At some time in your life," screamed Kate into the phone, "you have to exert yourself. You can't always hang around waiting for things to come to you. Sometimes you have to go after them, Holly. Why can't you try learning about the things Stein likes? Why can't you go to his next game and cheer for him?"

Why couldn't Stein learn how to build miniature firescreens? Why couldn't Stein become involved with afternoon television? Why couldn't Stein sit around buttering his salad? "I guess I could do that," I said morosely.

Kate tried to whip up a little enthusiasm describing the glories of Swann's Wood in January, but I had already had that nature series from Stein himself. Why should I have to change to be attractive? I thought. Why can't I just be me? Why pretend to be interested? Why fake enthusiasm?

But then I remembered that the real me was getting nothing but zeroes this season. School, coordination, boys, and college applications.

Perhaps what was required here was a new Holly Carroll. A swinging, athletic, enthusiastic, exciting Holly, paired with the best man in the senior class.

I pictured, instead, the best man in the junior class. Hunched over a muffin at the Pew, drinking in that beautiful sight of Nature at her best — butter melting.

I had never even thought of steam engines before Jamie mentioned his, but I'd been instantly interested.

". . . by ten o'clock in the morning," said Kate very firmly. I began to see a future for her in government, ramming unwanted programs down people's throats. "Be dressed properly, Holly."

"Okay," I said. "It'll be great." I thought of eight miles of frigid woods, and me on the seat of a snowmobile, the windchill factor molding my cheeks into new shapes. "Terrific," I told Kate. "I need the fresh air."

"Forget the fresh air," said Kate. "Concentrate on Stein."

Fourteen

My mother thought all this sounded like marvelous fun, and she smiled with delight thinking about the wonderful time I would have on my winter picnic. She even borrowed a snowmobile outfit (which is just a stylish adult-size snowsuit) from a friend of hers so I'd be properly dressed for the great adventure. The snowsuit was enormously bulky, a muddy pink color with lavender, white, and rose slashes down the leggings. Only color-blind people could even *think* about wearing it. I put it on and stared down at my doubled waist size.

"You look like a pro football player," said Christopher.

My father more or less rolled me into the

car to take me to Kate's and embarrassed me horribly by hanging around to chat with everyone about drugs. He's not very subtle. He'd heard the drug scene was getting bad again, and he wanted to know for sure so he buttonholed each of my friends and asked them where they bought drugs. Everybody said, "I don't buy," and "I don't associate with people who do," which was probably correct, but they would have said that to Dad no matter *what* the truth was. Everyone kind of stumbled around hoping not to be asked any more questions.

There was a bad moment when I thought Dad would say a blessing over the picnic basket and the thermoses, but the moment passed without a prayer (except mine to stop him!). My leg was strapped onto the snowmobile to prevent it from falling during the ride and getting tangled in the moving parts (a rather hideous thought), and thanks to Kate's maneuvering and Stein's basic lack of interest, I was settled behind Stein.

Actually it was easiest that way. I didn't have to pretend enthusiasm or utter little sentences of pleasure, because Stein is a doer, not a waster of time on meaningless chat. He just grinned, and we took off.

The engine made an appalling amount of noise. It was the sort of grinding, screaming mechanical racket that is totally offensive when you hear it in the distance, and yet when *you're* making it, and it's *your* noise, the racket is kind of comforting.

Deafening, though.

Others had used the path before us, and often. It was worn to a smooth road of ice. We'll all be killed, I thought, as Stein took the curves at speeds that would qualify us for an Olympic bobsledding team. I wondered if Jamie would come to my funeral.

We covered the eight miles to the waterfalls in mere seconds, or so it seemed. I hadn't even noticed Swann's Wood go by because I'd been too busy clinging to the grip. Stein and I arrived first. Either the others had less horsepower or they were more sane.

Stein stopped the engine and for a moment we just sat there, gazing at the waterfalls.

From between the scattering of evergreens came rays of winter sun, turning the ice to fire and the snow to stars. The waterfalls had frozen as they fell, in great gleaming icicles and enormous rounded nobs and tiny delicate plumes of ice sugar spray. Windblown snow and frost decorated the firs like patches of old lace. Every cluster of pine needles was thick with hardened snow in tight cruel balls, so that the pines looked decorated for Christmas by the icy hand of winter.

Near the skis of the snowmobile was a young fir no more than eighteen inches high. A filigree of ice clung to its tiny branches like a cathedral window star.

The sun reflected so blindingly I got tears in my eyes and had to blink to see.

Thank you, God! I thought unexpectedly. Thank you for so much that's beautiful. For the ice and the sun and the blue of the sky!

I'll be darned, I thought. There are still little pockets of religion in me. Who would have guessed?

Immediately, having made friends with God by complimenting Him on his terrific frost patterns, I began wondering what it would be like to talk to God about boys. "God, I think the mating pattern you allowed to evolve here is altogether too difficult. I want you to intervene in my life. Miracles will not be necessary. I want only a softening of the path."

I giggled softly, and Stein said, "Nice, huh?"

"Yes. Thanks for bringing me."

"Any time," said Stein, and he sounded very serious. As if I could phone during the next blizzard at three A.M. and Stein would gladly go out again to admire Nature's best with me.

I ached to be able to jump up. Circle the little pond. See how the frozen falls looked from behind the stand of birches. Look down into those animal prints immortalized in the crusted snow and guess who visited the pond.

The other snowmobiles roared. No, don't come! I thought. Leave me here to think about the little fir trees.

Three snowmobiles tore into the clearing. Stein yanked off his seatbelt and helmet and began unfastening me. Gary yelled a warning and slid to a precipitous halt inches away from us, Kate squealing with delight and Lydia yelling not to destroy the snowmobiles because she wanted her deposit back.

When I looked down, I saw that Gary's snowmobile had run over the tiny fir, destroying forever that tiny frosted work of art. There was nothing left now but a torn raw stub and a little mangled branch twisted in the skis.

Kate leaped off, and she and Gary hugged each other and looked self-consciously at all of us and then kissed lightly, and Lydia said, "Later, children, later."

"Why?" said Gary. "Best things first."

Susan and Ross claimed to be starving and dying of thirst, so they broke out the thermos of hot chocolate and the first bag of ham sandwiches. Stein, of course, shunned anything as pleasant as a hot drink and fished out a cold Pepsi. He even produced a plastic cup into which he dropped the tip of an icicle from the falls to ice his drink satisfactorily.

"I wouldn't use that for an ice cube," said Lydia. "It's probably frozen acid rain."

Everyone but me laughed.

"Say, what'd you think of the game?" said Stein at large. Everyone huddled around the food, talking about how exciting the game had been.

I could not believe they were sitting around talking about ice hockey and crunching taco chips. *It was all so beautiful!* Why weren't they gasping in awe and weeping because they hadn't brought cameras and offering their taco chips to the birds in homage to the best Nature had to offer?

I gazed over Stein's ample shoulders at the top of the falls, and for a moment watched a hawk circle lazily in the sky, a black and graceful creature against the deep, impossible blue of the sky.

The snowsuit was too warm. Who would ever have thought that Holly Carroll could get too warm? It mellowed me. I decided not to tell them that anyone who adored ice hockey was a barbarian and that Jamie Winter and Holly Carroll were the only outposts of civilization in a deteriorating world. I decided not to say that in my opinion a hockey stick was shaped exactly like a scythe — for slicing cheeks open, though, instead of reaping grain. I even decided to smile at Stein while he bragged about his chances at pro hockey and while I remembered Stein's opponents who had left the rink needing stitches.

I am practically a saint, I told myself. I am a big, big person.

I glanced down at the huge fat beast I was with the snowsuit on and thought ruefully that there were two ways to interpret "big."

"So, Holly," said Lydia, in that sharp, cruel tone she uses to introduce torment. "So how's dear little Jamie?"

Inside the suit I shriveled. Jamie was private. He was my fantasy. Lydia had no business introducing him here, for everyone to kick around like a downed hockey player. "He's fine," I said, trying to be casual. The blushes came and went on my cheeks like tides in the Bay of Fundy.

"Jamie who?" Susan wanted to know.

"Win — ter," said Lydia, as if those two syllables described something utterly comical.

"Jamie Winter?" repeated Susan. "You mean that junior?" She managed to make a junior sound as remote as an Afghan.

"Right," giggled Lydia. "Hollyberry here is crazy about him."

Kate jumped in. She was not so much being a pal as she was preserving my chances with Stein. "Drop dead, Lydia," she said crossly.

"You're like Hope Martin. Always nipping at somebody's heels. Stop starting rumors."

Susan had never once listened to Kate, and she wasn't listening now. "But Holly," she protested, looking at me with confused, surprised eyes. "Jamie's so young. I mean I'm practically two years older than Jamie. Don't you feel there's a tremendous gap? What could you possibly talk about?"

Everything, I thought. A thousand more things than I could ever talk to *you* about. I found myself wondering how the eight of us had ever managed to get together. I wasn't even sure any of us liked anybody else in the group very much. I certainly didn't like Lydia. And Susan was pressing me pretty hard. And if Kate kept trying to sell me on or to Stein I wouldn't like her anymore either. I said, "Actually, he's kind of a neat person."

I did it, I thought. I admitted it. I didn't pretend he's nothing but a clod to carry trays.

"She's really into cradle-robbing this year," said Lydia, smirking. "You know what else Hollyberry is into? Dollhouses." Lydia's distinctive laughter pealed out over the ice and vibrated in the woods. I considered violence.

Gary said mildly, "Jamie's six feet tall, Lyd. Little large for a cradle."

I forgave Gary for running over the fir tree.

And then Stein said (*Stein!*), "He *is* a neat person. He's kind of weird. Doesn't like sports even though he's got the build for them. Lifts weights, though, I think. But he can do anything mechanical. He's got a parts inventory in that garage of his like a J. C. Whitney catalog."

I forgave Stein for being a jock.

When God moved through Gary and Stein, He was definitely moving in mysterious ways.

Kate moved the conversation into the conditions on the various ski slopes, and pretty soon everyone was busy defending Loon versus Waterville.

I slid into a ski dream of my own . . . water skiing . . . off the West Coast, not down a mountain . . . under a hot California sun . . . with Jamie Winter.

Fifteen

My ankle cast was turning gray and ragged. I hated it now. It was a prison. I was even daydreaming about the moment the cast came off and I could have the glorious joy of kicking my foot and bending my ankle.

Dad drove me to school, because I found getting on and off the bus too difficult. We drove past my stop. The same kids were playing in a new layer of snow. The ones who usually leaned against parked cars and telephone poles were silently leaning. And Jamie was standing alone, staring off into the sky.

He didn't see us drive by.

Okay, I said to myself. The situation here is really very simple. I have determined that of all the boys in high school, I like him best. Unfortunately, I have alienated him. Justifiably, he no longer wants to attempt to be around me. I must retrieve the situation. I have to take the first step.

It sounded so easy, sitting there in the car next to my father, who could always take any step.

I saw myself trotting down the hall after Jamie, Hope on one side making remarks about how I couldn't even *talk* to a college man and Lydia on the other side, wanting to get tips on cradle-robbing. Meanwhile, a hundred other passing students were listening and giggling and pointing. Then I'd corner Jamie and explain that while I had said he was nothing but a young clod to carry trays, actually I adored him and could we go out? I'd pay, he wasn't to worry about that.

Then, of course, Jamie would look at me in absolute horror because all he *was* doing was carrying my tray. While Hope and Lydia laughed themselves sick, Jamie would flee down the hall, never to be seen again.

I no longer care about Hope and Lydia, I said to myself. They stink. Their boyfriends stink. All they want is to be unkind to other people and prevent other people from having fun.

I got out of the car and said good-bye to my father and went into the school with such determination I practically dug holes in the floor with my crutches.

And then, of course, I didn't so much as catch a glimpse of Jamie.

In English class I stared out the window, thinking about him. Our high school is built on a hill and from the top floor you can see through the tracery of naked trees to the college ski slope. It wasn't as crowded as on a weekend, but there were plenty of skiers. Tiny figures of scarlet, emerald, vibrant yellow, and royal blue danced against the white snow. Little feathered trees separated us. I daydreamed, half asleep. Was Jamie daydreaming of me? Or of hot buttered muffins in the Pew? Or of steam engines and college?

After school was the big meeting to organize the high school participation in the college's Ice Sculpture Festival. Tens of thousands of people come to the weekend, and for the last few years the high school has run children's games and small booths to raise money. This year our project was building a solar greenhouse off the biology rooms, and we needed several thousand dollars for materials. It had to be a lot more professional than in previous years, but it was a bad year for raising money;

what with the economy and inflation, people weren't going to be eager to throw dollars away on stupid little nothing prizes and games.

There were probably forty kids at the meeting. About half were seniors and the rest were a mix of freshmen, sophomores, and juniors. Jamie was one of them.

My heart jumped when I saw him. It seemed to me the whole room would turn around and see me breathing quicker, but no one did. Not even Jamie.

He was sitting on the far side of the room. On one side of him was an empty chair and on the other side sat a junior girl named Elsa Worrell.

My heart sank as quickly as it had risen. Elsa is a dreadful name, but Elsa's one of those perfect, sparkling little gamines who make you wish you, too, could be named Elsa and be a perfect, sparkling little gamine like that. Jamie was laughing with her. He was not going to look up and see me because the view of Elsa was far too nice to expect anything better to come in the door.

I could sit in the empty chair, I thought.

But Gary and Kate were already thrusting out a chair for me next to them. What if I went on by, and sat with Jamie, and he never even looked up from Elsa? Or looked up and was annoyed, and embarrassed?

It's only a *chair*, I thought, despising myself. This is just a dumb *meeting. What is the big deal?*

I sat down next to Kate. We were on the Executive Committee. I rather like committee work. It's always inside, I'm always good at it, and it keeps me busy.

"Okay, men," said the faculty advisor, Mr. Hastings. "Let's get this show on the road." How dare he call us men, I thought.

Hope said icily, "It happens that the chairperson, vice-chairperson, and two of the five committee heads are female, Mr. Hastings. Perhaps you should say, 'Okay, women.'"

Mr. Hastings chuckled agreeably. He was the sort of man my mother would loathe, because he could not quite believe women were ever in charge of anything. Why am I remembering my mother's opinion? I thought suddenly. I'm seventeen. *I* loathe Mr. Hastings!

"Ladies and gentlemen," amended Mr. Hastings.

I looked over at Jamie and Elsa. Elsa was not listening and didn't care. Jamie was looking at Mr. Hastings with a bored, scornful look that put Jamie on my side. I grinned to myself.

"We've got to have a large number of inexpensive activities this year," said Mr. Hastings. "Most of the booths have to be fifty-cent

143

booths. All the kids will want to do several things, but their parents won't be able to fork out two dollars each time. I figure we need at least ten booths or games."

Ten! I thought, overwhelmed.

"Is it too late to resign?" muttered Gary.

"Holly Carroll," said Mr. Hastings, terrifying me. "You did a good job on the Treasure Hunt last year. Want to do it again?"

Oh, that horrible Treasure Hunt!

I'd hidden the clues in snowballs, making up batches of snowballs for days in advance, keeping them outdoors and praying the temperature wouldn't rise. We'd hidden the snowballs all over the college president's backyard, among the shrubs and rocks and stone fences, and after each bunch of kids finished up and got their all-day lollipops, I'd have to run around hiding the next bunch. After two days of the festival, I was insane.

What have I been daydreaming about? I reproached myself. I have not given one moment's thought to what I could do this year instead.

"I'd rather do something else," I announced. I had to improvise fast. What are my natural talents? I thought desperately. Spanish . . . nice hair . . . hot weather. . . . "The college drink booths are pretty adult," I said. "A lot of cold drinks, plenty of coffee, some beer and some booze, but nothing for kids. I'd like to do a hot drinks booth. Small cups and small portions that cost very little. Hot chocolate. Hot buttered cider. Russian tea. Hot lemonade."

Ask me anything about hot drinks, I thought. I know 'em all. Actually I rather enjoy hot Dr Pepper, but it sounded too weird to mention, so I left it off the list.

Everybody thought that was a terrific idea. One of the freshmen thought small snacks would sell well, too. Plastic baggies with one doughnut, or two cookies, or a handful of popcorn.

Lydia agreed to do the Treasure Hunt. I revised my opinion of her yet again. She was certainly willing to work.

Darling gamine Elsa claimed to have an older sister who bred husky dogs. "Valery would give sled rides to little kids," she said. "Once around the block. They'd love that. We'd probably do real well."

Last year's big hit was ice-chasing, where the biggest boys took little kids on their shoulders and raced across the ice. The kids loved the height and the speed. It was a little hard on the shoulders of the skaters, but that's why they had those broad shoulders, right? Gary

Beaulieu and Pete Stein, as our best and broadest skaters, agreed glumly to do that this year.

One of the freshmen had a peculiar idea that everyone laughed at at first but then decided was really pretty good. She wanted to fill waterguns with colored water (and alcohol so it wouldn't freeze) and have children spray pictures on snow! They'd do a huge mural and each kid could pay a dime for his chance to empty a watergun and paint a blue tree or a red car.

"Take an awful lot of dimes to raise a thousand dollars," said Lydia.

"What we need," said Mr. Hastings, "is one really good thing that we can charge more for. One really super idea to swing the whole high school end of the festival around."

There was dead silence. Nobody had a single idea.

And then Jamie said, "Last year when I was in summer camp —"

"Camp!" moaned one of the senior boys. "Jeez, Winter, aren't you past that stuff yet? How old *are* you, anyway?"

Jamie's face tightened a little but he plowed on. I felt my stomach cramp up, worrying for him. Don't say anything dumb, I prayed.

"The camp owned a hot air balloon. It was beautiful. Bright deep red with two rainbows on it. The town had a Fourth of July carnival, and they used the hot air balloon for fundraising. The balloon doesn't actually take off. You keep it moored and release it to the limits of its ropes, probably fifty feet up, but that's enough for little kids. You can charge at least a dollar for that, because it's so unusual. You can also have someone there with a color Polaroid camera to take snapshots of each kid as he goes up in the air, and you always sell those to the parents."

"It's a nice thought, Jamie," said Lydia in her cruelest voice, "but we can't afford the balloon, we can't afford the fuel, and that also lets out the camera."

I hated her. I truly hated her. It was a terrible feeling, to have so much loathing for one person coursing through me. I almost hit her. I think the only reason I didn't was that Kate was sitting between us.

Jamie said, "I know a guy in Laconia who has a hot air balloon. His is emerald green with deep blue zigzags. It's really pretty in the sky. He —"

"Jamie," said Lydia, "who cares what color it is?"

Several people informed Lydia that she could shut up.

Jamie took a deep, controlled breath and said, "He'd be happy to do it for us. I asked him last week. He loves his balloon, he's proud of it, he loves showing it off, and he likes taking kids for rides. All we'd have to do is pay him back the cost of his fuel afterward, and by then we'd have the money in hand to do it. As for the camera, I also talked to the Camera Shoppe in town, and they agreed to let us have the film at cost and furthermore to let us pay for it afterward."

There was a moment of very impressed silence.

Stein said, "Winter, you're something."

"Yeah," said Jamie. "Well, there's one hitch."

"I knew it," said Lydia.

Gary kicked her for me. Lightly, but still, a kick. That Gary had possibilities, too.

"He wants two free ski slope passes for a weekend," said Jamie. Susan, whose father owns the Snowy Owl ski resort, immediately said, "Oh, no problem! My father always has a few passes on hand for special guests. That'll be our donation. My father was just complaining last night that I'd probably expect him to kick in something, and now I can tell him precisely what!"

We all laughed.

Suddenly the festival seemed like something we really wanted to do. The thought of that huge, many-stories-high emerald green balloon

soaring up in the sky, and the laughing, shriek-
ing children in its basket, made us all cheerful
and eager to get to work.

We broke into groups. By the time my committee had gotten its thoughts down on paper,
it sounded like a major conglomerate preparing for a takeover. I had had no idea providing
hot drinks for anywhere from zero to ten thousand people would be so difficult.

"Isn't winter cute," said one of my girls.

How anyone could find winter cute was beyond me. I made a mental note not to assign
this girl anything very demanding.

"He seems to like Elsa, doesn't he?" said
another girl.

Wrong winter, I thought. I looked up immediately. Jamie and several boys were trying
to decide what field they could use to moor
the balloon. Elsa was dancing over to offer a
suggestion, like a wood sprite, or a gazelle.
Jamie was smiling at her. The sweet, private
one-quarter smile we had shared in the cafeteria line.

My chest hurt again. I felt fat and ugly and
stupid, the sort of girl who would have to resort
to meeting men by computer, or in bars, or be
introduced in pity by superior female friends
with extra men around. Gloomily I wrapped
up my committee meeting. People began rushing off to catch the late bus or call for rides

home. Carpools were being worked out and mittens searched for. I shoved my stuff into my backpack (the general enthusiasm for carrying my things had long since worn off) and located my crutches. Hideous, evil instruments of torture. I jabbed them viciously into the floor. Elsa danced in front of me. I would have speared her except that she had done nothing to deserve it. It wasn't her fault I hadn't been bright enough to keep Jamie.

The group thinned out. Mr. Hastings called out little cries of good-bye and *au revoir*, and everyone sort of shuddered and wondered what the world was coming to when this was the best the faculty could muster. Jamie was slightly behind me, Elsa slightly ahead. I slowed down. "Hi, Jamie," I said smiling. My lips trembled. One dumb smile, I thought, it can't matter that much. Surely in seventeen and a half years I have at least learned to smile.

"Hi, Holl," said Jamie. He did not slow down. Either he was heading after Elsa, or he was avoiding me.

I said, "Jamie? Want to go to the Pew and have a muffin with me?"

Sixteen

If you ask for a hot drink at the Pew, you get it in a thick sand-colored mug, with a handle so thick you can't use it, and instead you wind your fingers around the mug and heat them off your hot chocolate. Ice water is served in an old mason jar. They've done that long before anyone thought that kind of thing was cute. It comes from the Depression, they'll tell you, when they couldn't afford glassware.

My jar had a pattern of grapes and leaves and vines running around it. I stroked the bulges of the grape cluster with my thumb and listened to Jamie's stories.

Sitting there with him I had this strange *complete* feeling. It was like the last piece you put into a thousand-piece jigsaw puzzle, or the final word you write in a twenty-five-page term paper. Seeing it done completes it. Seeing it finished wraps you up, too.

Seeing it right.

Jamie, I thought happily, is right.

We were talking about the ice sculptures. The wooden bases were beginning to go up on the fraternity lawns, and it was always fun to try to guess what on earth they might be. Ice sculptures are made from slush. A four-legged animal, for example, requires a simple saw-horse with a wooden headpiece around which you pour your slush, which you've mixed to your secret proportions in your snow and water pails. As you pour on the slush, you shape it with paddles and shovels and knives. After it's all up and frozen, you carve it with a hatchet and finish it off with a fine water spray that shines like glass when it freezes.

Some of the fraternities and some of the independent efforts (like Lydia's) were starting to go up, but so far there was just the wood and the beginnings of scaffolding for the really big ice constructions.

"Last year I remember Chi Rho had this huge thing on the lawn that I was convinced was going to be a stegosaurus," said Jamie.

"Chi Rho!" I said, laughing. "They won last

year with that giant fifteen-foot-long bunch of bananas."

"I know. When it was all done it was a perfect banana bunch, but while it was going up I was positive it was a dinosaur."

"Doesn't it make you think of Halloween?"

Jamie looked puzzled.

"The ice sculptures," I explained. "I mean, the effect of them all is sort of wild and crazy and sometimes attractive, but always so *ridiculous*. It makes you feel surprised at humankind for even *thinking* about it. Like Halloween. Who would believe there's actually a day set aside each year for people to pretend to be ghosts?"

We talked about the weirdness of other people. It was a topic good for hours. Jamie slid into discussing the solar greenhouse we'd be building over the summer, if we managed to raise all the money we needed during the Ice Sculpture Festival. "Solar greenhouse," he said scornfully. "I can't stand it when people say stuff like that. Even the biology teacher says it. I want to execute him. I mean, what other kind of greenhouse could it *be*? There's no such thing as a lunar greenhouse."

I buttered another strawberry muffin and handed it to Jamie. It was a purely selfish act. Any more muffins and butter and they'd have to shovel me out the door.

"Tomatoes in winter," said Jamie dreamily. "Instead of going to the vending machines for two-week-old chocolate-covered doughnuts or soft, ancient golden apples, we can go to the biology room and buy fresh tomatoes."

I wouldn't be there.

I would be a thousand, five thousand miles away.

I stared at Jamie for a moment and rethought my position. I could at least glance through the catalog of the University of New Hampshire. It was silly to write off a perfectly fine school without a thorough investigation. It was possible, I thought, regarding Jamie from a distance of two inches and planning how to reduce that to zero inches, that climate was not everything.

"Your lips are buttery," observed Jamie.

"I know. We can't go on meeting like this."

I thought he would kiss me, and I think he thought so, too, but at the last moment Jamie caught himself and pulled back an inch and instead drew a butter mustache on my upper lip.

We had each paid for a round of hot chocolate and muffins. Jamie said, "You have any more money? Because I am now down to fourteen cents, and we can't sit here forever not ordering because there's a line at the door."

I dug around among the used Kleenex and

scribbled memos and dried-out felt pens and discovered enough for two more hot chocolates.

"I'm not sure I can drink any more," said Jamie. "I'm going to float away."

"We can order it just to sit here," I said. "We'll look busy, at least."

We sat quietly waiting for the waitress to bring another set of drinks. "About the cafeteria the other day," I said. My stomach clenched around all the food I'd consumed at the Pew. Jamie looked at me without expression, waiting.

"I — I didn't mean to be rude," I said. "I loved it that you were there in line with me, Jamie. It was just — when Lydia — well, those girls started giggling and I felt so — I mean, that teasing about the older woman and the younger man thing really threw me."

Jamie nodded. "I haven't enjoyed it either."

I was astonished. "You got it, too?"

"What do you think all the junior boys were laughing so hard about when I went back to sit with them after Gary took your tray?"

"Oh, Jamie, how awful. I thought they were just laughing. I didn't think they were laughing at you."

"Oh, sure. All this stuff about how I expected you to show me Life and guide my weak little mind into Adulthood."

I almost chewed my lip off, hearing it. Jamie

had certainly deleted the actual words out of kindness to me. "Nobody said anything that bad to me," I said. "Just how I was into cradle-robbing along with dollhouses, probably was a case of severely retarded mental development, was warped, and required a similarly warped mind to keep me company."

We smiled. Tense, rueful smiles that didn't stay very well on our faces. Suddenly I wanted fiercely to be alone with Jamie. To hug away the accumulated tension of all the teasing and the uncertainty. We stared at each other over the table, and Jamie said, "Forget the hot chocolate. Let's go somewhere."

We were up from the table, and we touched fingertips as a preliminary. I shivered, thinking of the two of us being alone, but that was the highlight of it, I'm sorry to say. Cold weather once again reared its ugly head. We couldn't just saunter out and find a park bench. We had to locate our coats among the incredible pile-up at the door, figure out how to get our arms into the sleeves when we were being crushed by a dozen other couples eager for our vacated table, zip up, wind our scarves around our chins, pull on our two pairs of mittens, excuse ourselves twenty times while shoving through the crush, and then, outside in minus four degrees with the wind blowing, adjust to the shock and the sheer viciousness of the weather.

I dragged my crutches behind me, and we stood on the sidewalk crunching the pellets of rock salt. Jamie said, "Holly. This is the *pits*."

We both began to laugh. The wind was so cold it froze the insides of my lungs, and I had to put a hand over my mouth to soften the air before I breathed it in. Jamie grabbed my hand away and began dragging me right across the new-fallen snow onto the college campus. "Jamie," I protested, but the wind tore the words away. He pulled, I dragged, and the crutches made sinister streaks in the snow as I let them slide along the ground after me.

We came to a cluster of enormous, ancient fir trees whose branches swept the ground and the sky. Jamie walked straight into them, holding branches back for me, and there, inside, was a tiny clearing with a tiny stone bench and relief from the piercing wind. Jamie kicked snow and ice off the bench and sat me down on it, leaning the crutches up, and then sat down beside me.

I put my arms around him and felt nothing but layers of puffy cloth and padding. He put his arms around me and I knew the arms were there because I could feel the pressure, but that was all. I yearned for a hot sandy beach with a private lagoon just for two. I yearned for a heated car of our own, or at least a living room without a brother or a parent, or even membership in a fraternity with a warm sitting room and people who wouldn't turn the lights on.

No such luck.

We did find, however, that two faces pressed up against each other can at least keep the cheeks warm, providing entertainment and pleasure at the same time!

"You too cold?" said Jamie.

"I am always too cold. But don't let that stop you."

We laughed, and our breath hung in the air like clouds of love.

"You know something?" said Jamie. "Last year you were just some girl at the bus stop."

I nodded and touched him. "At first I just stood next to you because your shoulders were wide enough to block some of the wind."

"When do you get your cast off?" he said.

"Day after tomorrow."

"Friday, then. Let's celebrate. Where can we go together?"

We hugged each other and I thought, where *can* we go? Any place local means teasing, unless we stick to college hangouts like the Pew. Any place around here means being trespassed upon by the unfair, unthinking laughter of our friends.

"We could come to my house," I said, wondering uneasily how my brother would react to an evening of Jamie, and where we would sit, and whether we could possibly relax at all.

"No," said Jamie flatly. He and Christopher must have been more hostile than I had thought. "Your house?" I said tentatively.

"No. You don't want to see my parents in action."

"I don't?"

Jamie's face took on a hooded, private look. "I'm not the kind of son they had in mind," he said. "They're always mad at me, or embarrassed by me, or bewildered. We can't get along. I'm just never doing what they want."

"Do you ever give in?" I said. "Be what they want?"

Jamie laughed. "I might if I could ever figure out what they want. All I know is, it's not me. I can shrug it off now, though. College is in sight. Leaving home. My parents feel kind of temporary, as if I'm doing the last lap and pretty soon it'll be over and I can get out."

How awful, I thought. Why, I'll miss my family terribly when I leave for school. And they'll miss me. That's one reason they fight my going off so far.

We left the little circle of evergreens. The wind was biting as cruelly as ever. Jamie carried my crutches and took my arm, and we went slowly on the treacherous paths. Down on Little Pond at the edge of the campus, some little kids were out on the ice playing "Crack the Whip" in the growing darkness. The kid on the end got spun off the whip, and he slid in a crazy whirl across the ice. There was a shriek of happy laughter from the children who had skated too fast for him.

"Sometimes I feel like that," said Jamie.

"Like the last person on the whip?"

Jamie blew out an enormous cloud of hot breath into the frigid air. We walked through the cloud, and Jamie didn't answer me. "I know what we can do," he said. "There's a terrific old movie series at Dartmouth. Let's drive down there Friday night and see some silent films. Do you like popcorn and movies and stuff?"

Did I like popcorn and movies. "I also have a thing for chocolate-covered raisins," I said.

"At the same time?"

"If possible."

At least Jamie didn't condemn the practice out loud, although he did look a little pained around the edges. "I'll try to get the car," he said. It sounded as though getting the car would put Jamie in a war zone. I wanted to talk about Jamie's family, but I had the feeling he wasn't quite ready for that.

We came to Featherbed Lane and went

down the hill very slowly, so I wouldn't slip. The cast was exhausting me, and I ached all over, but I loved every minute of it. The feel of Jamie beside me, the grip of his arm, the way he pulled his steps shorter so he'd keep pace with me.

Far beyond us, on the opposite side of town, we could see one of the ski slopes. By day it was a smooth sheet of snow, but now, as the sun's rays vanished, each rise and swell of the mountainside cast a blue shadow on the white, and the infinity of ski and pole marks were like flaws on the surface of a moon.

Christopher opened the door. He raised his eyebrows, reminding me unpleasantly of Lydia. "If it isn't Jamie," he said mockingly.

"Come on in," I said to Jamie.

For one second Christopher blocked the door. He and Jamie stared at each other. I could not analyze what passed between them, but it sure wasn't brotherly love. "Yeah, Jamie," said Christopher, making the name sound idiotically girlish, "come on in."

I could have kicked him. Instead I took Jamie's hand and pulled him on into the living room where my parents were. Even Christopher wouldn't be rude if my father and mother were looking on.

"Why, hello, Jamie," said my father. "How are you tonight?" He shook Jamie's hand. It took Jamie completely out of the visiting-little-neighbor-kid category and put him into the man-who-dates-my-daughter category. Christopher was very annoyed.

"And how's Eunice?" said my mother. "Doing any better?"

We chatted about Jamie's sick aunt until Jamie said he had to leave. "What a shame," said Christopher, and my mother said, "Christopher, set the table, please." Christopher left, not very gracefully, and my mother and father found they had things to do upstairs. My mother gave me a tiny smile, as if she remembered how it was and we girls had to stick together.

It gave us a few moments alone to say goodbye, and as I kissed him and we looked at each other and felt an odd nervousness climb over us, so that the kisses got quicker and we were out of breath, I thought how neat it was that a person could love the whole world, and her parents, and needy migrants, and even (with an effort) her brat brother . . . and still have plenty of love left for a boy named Jamie Winter.

S*eventeen*

"Now," said the lecturer, "the first thing you must understand about silent movies is that they were never silent. Movie houses often had full orchestras, or at least a string quartet. Even the most rural movie house had its theater organ or its piano with organ pipes attached to double the notes on a flute and piccolo. The organ always had drums, thumps, foghorns, and sirens. Cowbells, tubas, traps, and xylophones could be built into the organ. Even newsreels were accompanied, as they were silent right into the nineteen-thirties."

I love to listen to people who love their subject. It's so neat to find out the things that interest people. Here was this elderly man up there at the organ (clearly leftover from silent movie days) and here lecturing was this young woman, who was entranced by the whole thing. Someday I will be giving lectures on something, I thought, and I will be so enthusiastic about my subject my listeners will be riveted to my words, just like this.

"The organist had to follow the script very carefully," she said. "He had to underscore the action, bridge unrelated film segments, approximate the gunshots, punctuate the fist fights, and sing sweetly beneath the love-making."

I thought of violins and cellos playing as the heroine fell back on her couch, swooning in the presence of the glorious man who had rescued her. I could see, now that I knew Jamie, how a girl could be tempted to swoon a little.

She held up cue sheets, showing us the sheet music with the cues for "Teddy at the Throttle," where Gloria Swanson was actually tied to a railroad track. The organist demonstrated what his instrument could do, and it was fantastic. Wild. Impossible. And funny. Everybody kept laughing with combined amusement and awe.

I ate another chocolate-covered raisin. Jamie popped another piece of popcorn into my mouth at the same time and watched, marveling, as I ate them together. "You're insane," he whispered.

"Happily so," I said.

"Sssssshhh," said the couple behind us.

The first film we saw was Douglas Fairbanks in "The Thief of Baghdad." I loved it. It was full of the sort of scenes you see on Saturday morning cartoons: ropes that stiffen on their own and become escape ladders; powder tossed in the air which becomes an army; magic carpets which soar up stairways. Everything in the sets was a marvel of sumptuous luxury and silken splendor.

I ate another chocolate-covered raisin. Jamie took the box of raisins and the box of popcorn out of my hands. I thought he planned to eat them himself, but instead he set them on the floor at his feet and handed me a napkin. I cleaned off all stray butter, salt, and chocolate, and Jamie took both my hands and began to draw snowflakes on them again. I could hardly watch the film.

We left at intermission.

"Why are we leaving?" said Jamie, willingly putting on his coat.

"It's going to last another hour and a half."

"And good films, too," said Jamie mournfully.

"We can go back if you want."

"Nope. All the back row seats are taken,

and the couples around us just came for the movies."

We began to laugh until we were gasping for breath, and we literally skipped out of the building. Lots of people saw us and raised their eyebrows or looked scornful, but we didn't know them, so they didn't count, and we didn't care.

The campus was a different one, and yet so much the same, one could hardly tell. We made angels in the snow, lying down in clean patches and swooping our arms — a whole row of them, as if we'd cut them from folded paper and set them hand to hand.

We rolled a snowman and chased each other around a granite wall and hid behind a Revolutionary War statue and pelted each other with snowballs.

Us. Jamie and Holly. Snow-haters.

It just went to prove that anything could be fun in the right company.

For supper we had pizza. It was the best pizza I had ever had in my life. The crust was as thick as my wrist and as crunchy and buttery as a French fry. There was so much pepperoni they had to stand it up vertically instead of laying it down on the sauce. We fed each other and held each other's cups to each other's mouths, and we never even noticed the rest of the world out there.

"When did your parents say you had to be home?" said Jamie.

"They didn't."

We kissed.

"When do they expect you, though?"

We kissed again.

"Soon."

We let the rest of the pizza turn cold and flat. "I guess," said Jamie finally, "that we'd better get going."

I wanted to refuse. I wanted to sit there forever, forgetting everything else. No more school, family, home, or festival committee. Just forever kissing, eating pizza, and laughing.

But the pizza house would close eventually, and we would run out of gas eventually, and my parents would notify the state police. Regretfully, I followed Jamie to the car. We drove several miles in companionable silence, watching the outlines of the trees and the mountains against the moonlit sky, seeing the way the snow revealed a frozen world.

"You know one reason why we had so much fun?" said Jamie quietly.

"Aside from the fact that you and I are perfect?"

"Aside from that," said Jamie seriously. "It was because no one knew. If we'd had the same movie program at home, and we knew that our friends — your group, my group —

167

were sitting in the rows all around us, we would have been stiff and self-conscious. We probably wouldn't even have sat together."

He was right. There was the solution of never dating at home, but that was expensive and depended on parents surrendering cars and snow not falling.

I pictured Monday.

There would be a lot of moments when, if Jamie and I were together, the entire school would trespass on us. Just getting to school. The whole bus. And homeroom. Hope and Stein and Zaweicki and the rest. Lunch. Especially lunch. Nobody in the history of our school has stepped over the invisible lines dividing one class from another in that cafeteria.

If I went to sit with Jamie and the juniors, I'd be a total alien, with not one word to say to them, and not one word for them to say to me. They'd tease Jamie unmercifully, and once we'd started it we'd have to keep it up or endure another whole subject of teasing.

If Jamie sat with me — well, he couldn't. There was no extra chair at my usual table. As for taking another table, the cafeteria was so crowded! I'd be shoving out people who usually sat there, and they'd have to displace other people, and every single person in the cafeteria would be aware of, and irritated by, Jamie Winter and Holly Carroll for disrupting things.

Which meant eating in the hall. Propping ourselves up against the walls by the vending machines. Facing all *that* traffic. Being twice as awkward because now we couldn't even sit down to eat.

Or we could just ignore each other during lunch.

But the teasers, the Lydias and the junior boys — they wouldn't ignore it.

I sighed.

"We ought to get it over with," said Jamie.

"Declare ourselves?"

"Yes."

I looked at him. Last year he'd been nothing. A little pesky jerk of a sophomore, tall but mentally shrimpy, like my rotten little brother Christopher. This year he was everything. I said, "I can if you can."

"Such enthusiasm."

"It'll be awful. A hundred people having their say. Being part of us. Saying things and thinking things and implying things."

Jamie shrugged. "You want to pretend we don't know each other, that's okay."

But it wasn't okay. We both knew it.

"No," I said firmly. "We'll do it. Eventually

they'll get bored and tease somebody else. Or, at the very least, summer will finally come and we won't have a cafeteria to contend with."

Jamie drove with one hand and held mine briefly. Then ice appeared, and he had to grip the wheel again. We lost traction for a moment and I held my breath, but we came out fine, without the slightest slipping on the ice.

Jamie muttered vile things about winter and how he hated it. But it wasn't really winter that was our problem right now. Oh, well, I thought. There's a whole two days of weekend ahead. By Monday I'll be so cemented to Jamie that nobody else's opinion will matter. I won't even hear Lydia, or see Kate, or notice Zaweicki.

Believe it.

E*ighteen*

There is no rest for the worried.

Saturday morning I woke up remembering the festival executive meeting. At ten A.M. we were meeting at the high school to produce whatever each of us had accomplished. We had to set up schedules, arrange advertising, be sure of ticket printing, decide on the cash and change needed at each booth, that sort of stuff.

Jamie's father needed the car. I told Jamie I would pick him up instead, and he said fine. Christopher put up a good fight to get our car, but my mother said that I had a better reason.

"Meaning Jamie?" said Christopher in great scorn. "Jamie's a wimp, not a reason."

"Shut up," I said, getting ready to crush a box of Rice Krispies in his face.

"You got any idea what kind of teasing I have to go through?" yelled Christopher. "You can't go out with Stein. No. You can't date a guy a guy could be proud of. Forget Stein. You have to date Jamie. A dumb *junior*. Who's just as weird as you are."

I threw the cereal at him, and Rice Krispies covered the kitchen floor.

"Defending your man with sugar cereal," said Christopher. "It suits. You two probably sit in some hot little corner somewhere talking about —"

My father said, "What are you, Christopher? Three years old? Four? Stop this. Holly, sweep the floor. Christopher, apologize."

"For what?" said Christopher sullenly. "She goes and embarrasses me all over the school and it's my fault?"

So I was not in the best of moods when I drove to Jamie's. It didn't help one little bit that he didn't come out to the car and I had to go ring the bell to get him. "Hello, Mr. Winter," I said, struggling to be cheerful. "Is Jamie ready?"

Mr. Winter just stared at me. "He's getting picked up by a girl?" said Jamie's father, as if he hadn't known women could vote, let alone drive.

"Yes, sir. I'm Holly Carroll, remember me from church? How are you, Mr. Winter?" I was determined to be courteous.

"Come on in. He isn't ready. Doing something for his mother."

We went into the living room, and Mr. Winter sat down and looked at me. I perched on the edge of the sofa and prayed for Jamie to finish his chores in ten seconds or less.

"So, how old are you these days, Holly?" said Mr. Winter. "Eighteen? Something like that?"

"Seventeen," I said.

"Must be a senior, huh? You go to that movie with Jamie last night?"

"Yes. It was very interesting. I'd never seen a silent movie before."

"At least he took you to the movies. I thought he'd probably want to show off his tractor."

Mr. Winter had a mean look in his eyes, like my eight-grade science teacher, who liked to spear people with his sarcasm. I said, "I'd like to see the tractor sometime, too."

"Jamie's still doing the stuff he did when he was a little boy," said Mr. Winter. "Hasn't grown up much. Toys. Steam engines. Makes you feel old, doesn't it, Holly?" He laughed.

Sometimes I got irritated with my father, what with his preaching and praying and hang-ups about labels on jeans and so forth, but my father would never, *never* ridicule me in front of my friends. Or in private, either. I shivered with anger at Jamie's father. He couldn't seem to get off the topic of Jamie. With each sentence he got more and more unpleasant.

Jamie came into the room behind his father. I could actually see the anger in him. Jamie had to look away and calm himself with a deep, slow breath. His mother actually moved between her son and her husband, as though they required her presence to prevent them from coming to blows.

"Let's get going," I said to Jamie, mustering a smile. "We're going to be late."

"Sounds just like your mother," observed Mr. Winter, making that sound like a criminal offense.

Jamie pulled on his gloves so roughly he might have been getting ready for a fight in the ring. I wanted to tell Mr. Winter what a creepy, crawly excuse for a human being he was, but instead I said, trying to be a peacemaker like my mother — like all mothers, I thought, glancing at Mrs. Winter — "Nice to talk to you, Mr. Winter," and got Jamie out the door ahead of me.

We got into the car, and I could feel Jamie hating that it was my car, that I was driving, and he had had to be picked up, and I had this prickle of fear that one year between our ages really *could* ruin things. I said, "You want to drive?"

He looked at me with flat, hooded eyes. "No."

That was the wrong thing to say, I thought. It won't help one bit to pretend that I'm the one who's younger and he's the one who's older. We are what we are, and we'll have to deal with what other people think of that, too. Jamie's right. It's my car, so I drive.

We didn't speak again.

When we walked into the meeting we were together and we were friends, but he was still rigid with his tension and I with mine.

Elsa danced over, as lovely and spritelike as ever. "Hi, Jamie!" she cried.

Jamie smiled at her. "Hi, Elsa," he said courteously. He took my hand and we sat down in the back, behind a row of seniors. They turned and looked at us, and we looked back at them and I smiled and said hello and everybody made a real point of looking hard at Jamie, and our hands, and *then* saying hello.

I hated them.

I hated them all.

It was nothing but time, nothing but months, nothing but age. It had nothing to do with whether Jamie was a terrific person or I was an interesting girl. It was stupid and pointless, and I hated them for it.

I have to get past this, I thought, drowning in loathing for the entire room, for Jamie's family, for Christopher. I can't go on feeling so full of anger toward people. I'll turn to acid.

And then I remembered that I was not in this alone. I was in it with — and because of — Jamie.

I looked over at him. Stupid, worthless Mr. Hastings was babbling on about the need to keep proper records of all cash transactions (as if we were all planning to keep improper records), and I held Jamie's hand and smiled at him and he looked back at me and immediately we both relaxed. I felt pleasure welling up in me again. The hatred was gone. The other kids were annoying, that was all. Kate turned around to ask something about my booth and I liked her again: she was still my best friend and somehow she would get used to Jamie and Jamie would get used to her.

Our hands lay soft on each other, his larger than mine, rougher, with blackened marks on the pads of his fingers where he had not quite gotten off all the grease from the last time he'd worked on his steam engines.

The meeting ended, and people drifted out. Several people made remarks or looked askance at us, but it didn't bother me terribly. I hoped Jamie felt the same way. We found ourselves walking automatically toward the Pewter Pot, for food and privacy. Remarkable how much privacy there can be in a place jammed with strangers.

"Is your father always like that?" I said.

He shrugged. "If you think he was hard on you, or me, you should hear him lace into my mother. A few years ago I even talked to your father about it."

So that was it.

"Your father's a pretty decent person, you know," said Jamie. He was sort of shy about saying it, as if my father might be my private property and I might not want Jamie having any of him. "I couldn't think of anyone else to ask, anyhow."

"Ask what?" I said.

"Basically, why Mom didn't just leave my father. I mean, why on earth would she want to stay and put up with that? All the time jeering and taunting. *I* didn't want to stay with him, see. I wanted to leave, and that meant she had to leave, too. And you know what your father said?"

"No." I tried to picture them. Jamie telling my father how rotten his family was; my father answering.

"He said never to overlook the possibility

that my mother really loves my father. Meanness and all." Jamie shook his head.

"You'll be out of it in a year and a half," I said.

"No. You never really get out of it. It's my family. He'll always be my father and she'll always be my mother, and he'll always be cruel and she'll always take it."

Jamie had not turned out in the least like either of them. "You survive awfully well," I said. I remembered that indeed that was just how he had answered my father. *I'm surviving.* "I sure am glad I don't have any problems like that."

"If you ask me, Christopher could be as bad to live with as my dad."

I laughed. "How come you two don't like each other?"

"I don't know. I've never been able to stand him."

"He's improved in the last few years," I said, offering a defense.

"Not measurably."

I laughed again. "In years past, I just steered around old Christopher, and I guess I can get back into it. But really, I think he'll get used to us and just ignore us."

"At home, maybe," said Jamie. "You should hear him in math."

"To you?"

"To the class. About me."

"Perhaps we could murder him," I suggested.

Jamie grinned. "A fine example of sisterly feeling."

"My familial love comes and goes."

All of a sudden we were kissing across the table. The waitress said, "I like smooching, too, kids, but we don't rent the table for that. You gonna order or you gonna leave?"

"We gonna order," said Jamie, and we laughed, and wrapped our ankles around each other's, hugging our feet, and ordered.

Nineteen

For the first time in six weeks I rode the bus to school Monday morning. There were so many congratulations and jokes to be made on the ankle that bent normally and the ragged cast that was finally off that hardly anyone even noticed Jamie grinning at me through the crush. But when we got on the bus, Kate headed for our usual seat. "Gosh, I'm glad you're back on the bus," she said. "I hated sitting alone. Come look at my new list of lipstick names. I've had some super-beautiful ideas."

She was sliding over into her seat at the same moment that Jamie, one row back, was sliding into his. I literally didn't know what to do. I just stood there, staring helplessly at the two vacant seats.

"Siddown!" yelled the driver. "I can't drive with you kids standing up. Now siddown!"

I sat down. With Jamie. "Kate?" I whispered through the seats. "Kate, can I look at your lipstick list during English?"

Kate stared at me. Emotions fluttered over her face like little birds. I could see her thinking, *Jamie's that serious! And I didn't know. My best friend didn't share that with me. She'd rather sit with him than with me. Jamie!* Kate swallowed and said, "Sure, Holl." She turned around and sat very still, facing the front of the bus, ignoring us.

Jamie said, "You could ride backward and show it to us both now. I still feel hurt that you don't want to use my suggestions."

"What suggestions?" said Kate, her back to us.

"Isopropyl Lanolate was one," said Jamie.

Kate giggled. "Don't you remember I told you that lacks rhythm, Jamie? You have to think of things like Bronzeberry Glacier, or Snow and Honey. Or Maple Syrup Icicle."

"Get your homemade Vermont Farm Lipsticks here," said Jamie.

Kate turned around now and frowned at

us over the seat top. "What's the matter? You don't think those names are sophisticated enough?"

"Just Maple Syrup Icicle," I said. "That one doesn't fly."

We talked lipstick names all the way to school, with Kate twisted up in the seat to talk backward to us. We got off the bus together, and Hope and Grey pulled up behind us and began their usual passionate departure for the day. I tried to get indoors before Hope saw me with Jamie, but I failed. "Why, Holly Carroll," said Hope, as if I were the last person she would expect to find in high school. "And Jamie." As if Jamie were my little boy with the runny nose.

Hope turned to Grey. "You can inform Jonathan that it's just as well he didn't pursue Holly, Grey. She can't master speech with an adult, so she turns to kids like Jamie."

I have to give that old Grey credit. He didn't actually rebut Hope's remark, but he did look very uncomfortable about it. He sort of saluted Jamie in embarrassment and scooted back to his car, looking distinctly nonsuave.

"Hope?" said Jamie. "Do you have an ulcer?"

"No. Why?"

"Because if you did I would harass you so

much it would start bleeding, and maybe you'd bleed to death," said Jamie.

At least twenty people heard that and cracked up laughing.

"A little crude, perhaps," said Kate. "A little lacking in the milk of human compassion, but nevertheless succinct and to the point."

Everybody broke up laughing again.

Jamie took off for his homeroom.

Kate said to me, "For real, huh?"

I flushed a little. "He's terrific, Kate. You'll like him."

"Okay. I still think you're crazy. Stein likes you. But if that's what you want, it's not my business."

Such a roaring succession of compliments on the man of my choice. Oh, well. At least Kate's opinion wasn't as low as Hope's.

I walked on down the hall to the pit of my homeroom, catching up, of course, to old Hope herself. Hope spent homeroom telling people about how childish I was, how drastically immature, how painfully young.

Stein said, "Somebody put a leash on her. She's biting ankles again."

Hope stopped immediately because the boys all laughed when Stein ordered it. "Stein," I said, "you're a prince."

"True," he said, and grinned at me. He does like me, I thought, in just the way I like him.

I survived all twelve minutes of homeroom and was relatively intact by the time lunch began.

All my fears piled in on me again. It's just lunch, I said to myself, it's nothing but a warm and nasty pimiento cheese sandwich, it is not World War III. Jamie managed to get in line with me, but his whole crowd of junior boys got in with him, laughing and shoving and being thoroughly worthless. Ahead of me were Lydia and Gary and Kate and Susan and Stein. There was no other place than the hot lunch line where those two groups of people would meet.

If only we were in a hot climate.

We could take our trays and walk romantically outside. Sit in the shade of a jacaranda tree. Watch a tennis game. Contemplate our tans.

But it was snowing again, and six degrees with a wind from the northwest. Perfect for ice festivals. A little rough for tête-à-têtes.

Jamie twisted his huge, old muddy shoe around mine, and I twisted my maroon boot around his. We were trying to have a cafeteria-line date in spite of the odds against it, but the enemy won.

"What are you doing?" demanded Lydia. "Going in for wrestling?"

One of Jamie's classmates laughed insanely.

"Leg wrestling first," he said ominously. "And then —" He made a really obscene suggestion for what came next. I ceased to breathe. Up ahead of me Kate's shoulders sort of tightened, and Lydia snickered. Susan turned around to stare at Jamie as if debating whether or not that sort of activity really was Jamie's sort. I couldn't see what Jamie did but the junior boy said, "All right, all right, don't get hot, I was just joking."

We got to the head of the line, and I felt as if my whole life were at stake. I kept telling myself it was nothing but a lunch, a dumb lunch, and all the time I kept wishing either Jamie and I or else everybody else would just disappear.

Gary Beaulieu paused with his loaded tray. He had four meals on there. I knew they were all for him. He and Stein eat like horses when they have a game. "Jamie," he said, "sit with us? I couldn't get permission to use the soccer field. We're going to have to come up with something else. We gotta work out where to put that hot air balloon now."

I could have kissed old Gary. At least we were over the hump of putting Jamie with the seniors.

We followed Gary to our old table. Gary, still talking, began kicking chairs around with his feet, hooking one from an adjacent table and shoving it in at the end of our table. ". . . thanks to you," he said. "Too bad we can't put advertising on the side of the balloon. Mr. Marchette over at the ski school says he's seen balloons that advertise magazines, like Forbes Capitalist Tool and the Prune Balloon."

"I suppose we could hang a sign on the edge of the basket," said Jamie, "but the silk itself has to be printed like that before it's sewn together."

"Where do they make those things?" said Gary.

"My friend got his in North Carolina. The weather down there is a little better for ballooning than it is around here."

"I'm going to hit up the Edelweiss Shop," said Gary. "It's such a good idea we have to capitalize on it. Or maybe Outdoor Traders. Anyway, I ought to be able to sell some kind of advertising for the balloon."

Jamie was between me and Gary, and on the other side of me was Stein and across from Stein was Kate. An impregnable position. Lydia arrived last. "What have we here?" she said, in her most snide voice.

Kate said, "Holly's boyfriend. Now shut up and eat your potato chips."

Susan said, "What I worry about are those husky dogs. Just looking at their crazy blue eyes you know husky dogs are insane. Imagine how they'll react to that great whoofing noise the hot air balloon makes.

"We'll just warn Elsa's sister," said Jamie. "She raises the dogs, she ought to be able to handle them."

"She's probably insane, too," pointed out Susan, "just being the type to raise them."

"Let's not go looking for trouble," said Stein. "Jamie, what are you buying these days?"

I thought this was the cue for some sort of teasing remark, but Stein seemed to be genuinely interested in whatever Jamie was buying these days. "I had my eye on an antique threshing machine," said Jamie, "but my parents wouldn't let me bring it home."

Stein agreed that parents were a nuisance. "*My* parents are trying to stop me from playing hockey. How's *that* for a kick?"

Kate said, "You know what's the best gift of winter?"

"The best gift of winter," repeated Susan, smiling. "What?"

"Weather forecast. Perfect temperatures for the ice sculptures, and no wind and no snow predicted to bother the hot air balloon. It's going to be a fabulous festival."

They went on chattering.

I felt peaceful. The cafeteria was full of shouting and noise and the clatter of trays and chairs being shoved under tables. My friends were friends after all, and I had not died during lunch, I hadn't even suffered. After all that agony, it *was* nothing but a few months, nothing but time, that separated Jamie and me.

I nudged Jamie.

"What?" he said, smiling.

"The best gift of winter," I said, very quietly and privately, my words hidden by the noisy talk of the rest of the table, "is you."